Desperate Measures

D0928899

Laura Summers grew up in South London and was a teacher before turning full time to writing. She has written scripts for many popular children's TV series, including *The Story of Tracy Beaker*, based on the stories of Jacqueline Wilson.

Desperate Measures is her first novel. The idea came from the observation there were very few characters with learning disabilities in children's books and the reality that one of her own children is disabled. The result is the creation of Rhianna and her sister Vicky: two very individual teenagers, one of whom happens to have learning disabilities.

Laura now lives in North Devon with her husband and children and, when not writing, loves to draw and paint.

Desperate Measures

LAURA SUMMERS

PICCADILLY PRESS • LONDON

To my family

With thanks to Lucy, Gaia and Anne

First published in Great Britain in 2010
by Piccadilly Press Ltd,
5 Castle Road, London NW1 8PR
www.piccadillypress.co.uk

Text copyright © Laura Summers, 2010

A catalogue record for this book is available
from the British Library

ISBN: 978 1 84812 050 1 (paperback)

1 3 5 7 9 10 8 6 4 2

Printed in the UK by CPI Bookmarque, Croydon, CR0 4TD
Cover design by Simon Davis
Cover illustration by Sue Hellard

Chapter 1

My name is Rhianna Jane Davies but my twin sister Vicky always calls me Re. I'm much taller than her but because she's forty-seven and a half minutes older than me, she's always trying to boss me around. When she tells me I've spilt my yogurt or put my T-shirt on back to front or something, I pretend I can't hear her and start singing really loud. Then I call her a sticky slob bottom and that really gets on her nuckets. She makes that face – the one where her mouth stretches out sideways and her eyes go up in triangles. She looks like she's going to explode but she hasn't so far. Most times she just yells at me and stomps off, banging the door so loud it makes my ears hurt.

It's our birthday tomorrow. We're going to be fourteen and I can't wait. I've made Vicky a card – it's got sparkly stuff stuck on it and some tinsel I found in the cupboard under the stairs. Jamie helped me spell the words and wipe off all the glue so Vicky can open it. Jamie's our little brother. He's got black caterpillar eyebrows and hair that sticks up like a loo brush. He's ten and always getting into trouble.

I'm not in the same class as Vicky because I have lessons in the Special Unit. It's not very special, except the ceiling's got a big brown stain because the roof leaks when it rains. Vicky gets really angry if the other kids say nasty things to me. Once when Charlene Slackton called me Der-Brain, Vicky went up to her and said she'd like to see her survive for nearly an hour without enough air to breathe. That's what happened when I was born you see. I was coming out of my mum's you-know-what and I got stuck. Probably because I've got really big feet. Size eights. Vicky only takes fives and Jamie's a pidgy four and a half.

Chapter 2

It must have been five o'clock this morning when Rhianna woke me up. Five a.m. and she's all excited and yelling in my earhole.

'Vicky, come on Vicky, let's go down and see what presents we've got!'

I ignored her for as long as I could but when she ripped my duvet off and started bouncing up and down on my bed, all nine and a half stone of her, that was it. I'd had enough. She drives me bonkers. It's really weird – although she's got this amazing memory for things that happened years ago, she's got absolutely no idea about time – we're talking 'big hand' and 'little hand' here and even then she still hasn't got a clue. Most days she doesn't even know what day of the week it is or whether she's just eaten her breakfast, dinner or tea.

'Get off, Re! Go back to sleep!' I yelled.

But she wouldn't. She disappeared off downstairs to wait for Mr Postie. After twenty minutes there was no sound, so I went down to check she hadn't electrocuted herself or flooded the kitchen, or both. She was sitting on the doormat poking a dead daddy-longlegs.

'Come on, Re. Back to bed . . .'

'But Dad might have sent us something.'

'The postman won't be here for another two hours and even then he . . .'

I stopped and looked at her, sitting awkwardly on the mat, her legs crossed like a badly jointed puppet's and her wide grey eyes fixed expectantly on the letterbox. I didn't like to burst her bubble but things were different now. We were on our own. Without Mum and Dad I mean. Mum died just over two years ago and Dad . . . well . . . I don't want to go into that right now but he's not around any more. It's not all bad news though. We've been fostered by a lovely couple called Paul and Sarah for the last eight months. It's meant we've had to go to new schools but at least we're finished with all those manky children's homes. Now they really were the pits.

I could see Rhianna wasn't going to budge. In the end I gave up, pulled the throw off the settee and tucked it round her because her hands and feet were going bluey-purple. I went into the kitchen and made a cup of tea, wondering whether Matt had got me a birthday card.

Matt is this gorgeous boy in my form. Don't get me wrong, he isn't actually my boyfriend or anything . . . but he was meeting me at the end of the road this morning and we were walking up to school together. My friend Rosie said I should consider myself as having engaged his attentions. (It's OK – she's a bit weird, she talks like that.) Anyway, you should have seen the look on Charlene Slackton's face when she heard about it; she was sooooo jealous because he's rated the hottest boy in the whole of Year Nine. And he likes me. Me! Vicky 'Shrimp-Face' Davies.

Maybe I should explain. I'm really short. I have curly red hair that never does what I want it to (think ginger fuzzball), I blush when I'm embarrassed (too much of the time), have tons of freckles (say no more) and wear flat sensible shoes for school (thanks to Sarah). Since I've been at this new school I've made just one friend – Rosie – who's the school boffin and reads Jane Austen novels instead of teen mags. Charlene has long blond hair down to her waist, wears really trendy clothes and high-heeled shoes that she can hardly walk in and everyone who's anyone would chop their right arm off and beat themselves with the soggy end if it meant they could be in her gang. Except Rosie of course, who wouldn't see the point, and me . . . maybe. Anyway, I blew my chances of ever being one of Charlene's best buddies when she teased Re and I told her exactly where to go.

Which reminds me. Rhianna had better not kick up a fuss when she finds out she's got to walk to school with Jamie today. I'm not looking after her. Not today of all days. She's such a big kid. She'd spoil everything. She always does.

When the postman finally came, there was a letter for Sarah and a few cards for us. Re was opening all our cards as Paul and Sarah came downstairs.

'Aren't you going to sing us both happy birthday?' I joked.

Sarah smiled and was about to say something but suddenly grimaced, sucked in her breath and rubbed her hand across her stomach. 'Oooowww.'

'You all right, love?' Paul asked. Sarah nodded and forced a smaller, tighter smile.

'I'm fine. But I think we're going to have a karate champ on our hands!'

Paul and Sarah have been the best thing to happen to us in a long while and now things are set to get even better. Although she's pretty ancient (she must be at least forty-three) Sarah's going to have a baby! They were over the moon when they found out – and so were we when they told us we weren't going to be moved on again. Hooray! They'd decided they would carry on fostering us, baby and all. Jamie and I want it to be a boy, Rhianna's holding out for a girl but Paul and Sarah say they don't care as long as it's healthy. So in a few months' time, we'll all be up to our armpits in nappies, bootees and baby sick, and believe it or not, we're all looking forward to it.

Rhianna was busy sorting through the cards. She desperately wanted one with a *14* badge. There was a card for each of us from Mrs Frankish. She's our social worker but Jamie's managed to convince Re that she's really a witch because she's got a mole on her face with hairs growing out of it. She'd spelt Rhianna's name wrong, as usual, but had boosted our card count by fifty per cent. There was nothing from Dad. When Re realised, her big grey eyes started to water and her large moon face crumpled.

'Never mind, Re,' I said, hugging her as she towered over me. 'Maybe there aren't any postboxes where he is.'

Paul looked up from buttering some toast and I felt my face reddening. 'Dad's doing a really important job delivering medicines and food to all those refugees,' I whispered to her when he was out of earshot. There was no way I wanted Rhianna or Jamie understanding where Dad really was. I didn't want anyone to know. It was a big black secret and it was better it stayed that way. When we first arrived at Paul and Sarah's, I sneaked a look at our paperwork while Mrs Frankish was busy chatting. I scanned the pages, detailing all the children's homes we'd been in and then saw the large, hastily scribbled words – *No contact with dad*. I remember feeling a huge wave of relief as I realised that was it; no further explanation was needed: Mrs Frankish had rubbed him out of our lives.

Re gave me her card and I made a massive fuss over it. I knew she'd been making it for about two weeks but I pretended it was a big surprise. It was like the sort of thing Jamie used to bring home from playschool, everywhere smudged with paint and big, wonky letters. I gave her another big hug and told her it was my best card. She looked so proud, I knew she believed me. Then I gave her a present, a Furby – she's wanted one for ages – and, thinking maybe this was a good time, I broke the news that she'd have to go to school with Jamie today.

Whoa! Big mistake. You'd have thought I'd told her she had to stick her head in a bucket of worms, she made such a fuss. Talk about an instant thunderstorm.

'I hate you!' she yelled. 'I was going to give you one of my Barbies for your present,' (she'd cut the hair off them both playing hairdressers last week) 'but I'm not now. You . . . you . . . conkhog!'

Don't ask me what a conkhog is, I haven't a clue. It's just one of Rhianna's special words she reserves for when she's losing it. She snatched back her card and sat on it. Paul tried to calm her down but I know what she's like when she gets in a paddy. It's better to leave her alone or it just gets worse. Anyway, I thought, I'll make it up to her tonight. Sarah had let me get her a cake – it cost a packet and looked totally naff with bright blue icing but it had a picture of her favourite boy band on it. So I went out into the hall, got my school bag and slipped quietly out the front door.

Chapter 3

All boys are vom. And boys called Matt are the vommiest of all. She could have let me come. I wouldn't have said anything. I could have walked behind them – they wouldn't have known I was there. I can walk really quietly even when I've got my clodhoppers on.

I hate walking to school with Jamie. He said we had to go past one of the houses really quickly in case some boy saw us and he did so Jamie shouted 'Leg it!' and we had to run. He nearly pulled me over because we were going so fast. I got a stitch but Jamie still wouldn't stop. We ran up to Sam's house (that's Jamie's friend) and banged on the door. Sam's mum answered and the boy ran off shouting that he and his mates were going to beat Jamie up after school. Jamie yelled back that he didn't care but his face went all chalky like it did when Mrs Frankish told us that we weren't allowed to live with Dad any more.

We went back the way we came and up to the woods. Jamie and Sam showed me their camp. It's a secret though so don't tell anyone. Only Jamie, Sam and me know about it. They've made a little den out of branches and ferns. It's lovely inside, all green and fuzzy.

We spent ages messing about. Jamie and Sam were making the den bigger and I made some delicious stew. It's ever so easy. You just get a load of leaves and mud and stuff, put them in a hole in the ground and mix it all up with a long stick. I didn't have any water so I used my break-time drink. I had to pick out a couple of boogeybugs but it looked all right.

'Let's come here again tomorrow before school,' said Jamie.

'Yeah. I'll knock for you both really early,' Sam told us.

When Jamie dropped me off at the school gates everyone had already gone in. Mrs Edwards was standing outside the Unit talking to Vicky.

'Where the hell have you been Rhianna Davies?' Vicky shouted. Her eyes were all red and puffy. I looked down and counted the lino squares. I wasn't going to tell her about Jamie's camp. Tough titty if Mrs Edwards told her off. She shouldn't go off with stinky boys, should she?

Mrs Edwards said there was no harm done and Vicky had better get to her class. We did cooking all morning and I made cheese straws. Except you couldn't blow through them. They just go soggy.

When it was home-time I saved Vicky my three biggest

cheese straws. I wrapped them up in some foil Mrs Edwards gave me but Vicky said she didn't want any. She said she was still cross with me about this morning.

We were walking down the corridor when suddenly she stopped and turned round and started staring at the noticeboard.

'What's the matter Vick?' I asked but she didn't say anything. Then this tall boy came up to her and she went all red. Even her neck. She looked like a big red tomato.

'You look like a big red tomato Vicky,' I said. She didn't answer so I said it again but much louder this time. 'Vicky. I said you look like a big red tomato.'

'Shut . . . up,' she said with her teeth gritty, then she grinned at the tall boy all smiley-toothy.

It was Manky Matt. He saw my cheese straws wrapped up in the foil and said, 'What's that then?' I said cheese straws and he said could he have one. I didn't want to give him one but then I thought if he was my friend too, Vicky would let me walk to school with them tomorrow. He took two. He was only supposed to take one. Do you know, some people can't even count.

'You must be Vicky's cousin,' he said with a grin.

'We're sisters,' I said. 'Twins.'

Vicky was looking at her shoes.

'Oh,' he said. 'Vicky told me you were cousins . . .'

I heard her call after me but I didn't stop. I ran past the toilets. Charlene Slackton was outside, leaning on the wall talking to another girl. They screeched with laughter and Charlene stuck out her foot and the other girl said 'Loser' as I tripped up.

I was scared so I got up straight away and ran out of the entrance, through the gates and up the road. Vicky was shouting at me to stop but I didn't. I ran across the road. A car slammed on its brakes and the driver opened his window and shouted rude words at me.

Vicky caught me and pulled me back on to the pavement. She was really angry. 'You stupid idiot! You could have been run over!'

I pulled away from her. 'Leave me alone.'

'You know you're not allowed to go home on your own. You know that!'

'I hate you Vicky.'

'Good.'

'I wish I didn't have a sister. Especially a horrible twin sister.'

'The feeling's mutual.'

'You're mutual too . . . And smelly. Really really smelly!' I shouted at her.

We turned round and started walking home. I didn't want her walking next to me so every time she caught up I raced on. It really got on her nuckets. Serve her right. I wished she *was* my cousin. Then I wouldn't have to see her every day or share a room with her and have to listen to her snoring like a hippo every night.

When we got home Mrs Frankish was there. I asked her if she'd got me a present but she just sort of mumbled something. Paul came in looking all serious. Mrs Frankish said she'd got something very important to talk to us about. I told her I knew all about having babies already because of Sarah and it's really gross and no way was I ever making one. Paul sat down and told us that Sarah was in hospital. I asked if she was having her baby now but Mrs Frankish said it was much too early. 'So what's she doing then?' I said. Mrs Frankish said Sarah wasn't well and she was going to have to stay in hospital so they could keep a really close eye on her and the baby to make sure everything went OK. Paul kept shuffling about and saying he was sorry and then he told us he wouldn't be able to look after us for a while. I said was Sarah going to go away like Mum and he just started crying so I gave him my last cheese straw. He didn't eat it, he just kept looking at it and rolling it on the table like it was a twig or something.

Jamie burst in. He was all out of breath and he had blood on his face. He wiped it off with his sleeve but no one noticed except me because they were all crying except Mrs Frankish who was patting Paul's hand. Some of her nail varnish was chipped off so I had a good look but I didn't see any black. (Witches have black fingernails, Jamie told me.) Jamie said, 'What's up?' and she explained it all over again. When he asked who we were going to stay with, Paul just looked at Mrs Frankish and didn't say anything.

Jamie said no way was he going back to those rude word, rude word, very rude word children's homes. Mrs Frankish didn't even tell him off for swearing – she just sighed and said we couldn't go back there anyway because they were all full up. I asked, 'Where we going then?' and there was another big silence. Then Mrs

Frankish said that there was a lovely school that I could go to, and they had a swimming pool and you didn't go home when lessons were over, you stayed and had a sleep-over every night. I always wanted to have a sleepover but my friend Maxine can never come to stay because she has funny fits when she goes to sleep. I said great, I can't wait but then Vicky said no way was I going to be parcelled off like that.

'But you'll come too Vick,' I said, 'and Jamie. I'll tell them you don't like swimming.'

I've got my five-hundred-metre badge. Vicky says she can swim but she can't – I've seen her and she puts her foot down all the time.

Mrs Frankish said they couldn't come because it wasn't suitable for them. I asked why not and she said it was a special school. I told her Vicky and Jamie were special and she just nodded and said of course they were. But then she said she had managed to find two families who could each foster one child for a while. Mrs Frankish said she was sorry but it was all arranged. We were going tomorrow.

Chapter 4

I followed her out of the room.

'Tomorrow? Tomorrow! No way!' I yelled. 'You can't do this to us!'

'I've been chasing round half the afternoon trying to find places for you all,' she said with a sigh. 'Believe me, we're lucky to have got what we have.'

'We? WE! It's not we, it's nothing to do with "we"! *You're* not going to be shoved away with some horrible family or carted off to some manky school where you don't know anyone and no one knows you.'

She turned and looked at me. 'There's no point in making a fuss, Vicky,' she said with that 'I'm a caring and concerned social worker' look slapped across her face. 'There *is* no other option.'

I could feel the anger boiling up in me. She must have

realised because then she said, 'I'll just leave you to have a little time out on your own to calm down a bit, then you'd better start getting your stuff together.' She started to walk out but stopped at the doorway.

'Oh,' she said casually, like this sort of thing happened all the time, 'I've got some bin bags if you haven't got enough cases.'

Bin bags! That just about summed it up. She was shuffling us around as if we were no more than a few bags of rubbish to be tidied out of her way.

Well, what about what *we* wanted? Didn't that matter? That stupid woman had so much power over us. It was criminal. And what was worse, she pretended that everything she did was in our best interest or some other rubbish. She didn't really give a monkey's. Once she finished her shift and had gone home, as long as we were neatly filed away in her out-tray, I bet she never even gave us a single thought.

I didn't want to stay with some family twenty miles away, I didn't want to leave my school and I didn't want to leave Matt. It wasn't fair. I'm not going, I thought. And I'm not leaving Rhianna and Jamie either. Jamie was always in trouble; if he was shoved somewhere else he'd really go off the rails and Rhianna was such a baby it would be cruel. She might be a right royal pain in the butt ninety-nine per cent of the time, but she was my sister and she needed me.

But what could I do? I grabbed my mobile and pressed Rosie's number. I hadn't known her for long and she was pretty odd sometimes but she was my friend and boy, was I a friend in need. Maybe she could help; after all she was supposed to have an IQ of three billion or something. The second I heard her voice, I realised I was living in cloud cuckoo land. How could I have been so stupid? How could I have possibly said, 'Hey Rosie, will your parents put me up for a bit? Oh, and there's my delinquent little brother and my brain-damaged twin sister too . . .' So I wittered on about Matt and she promised to lend me a book of seventeenth-century romantic poetry. I didn't get round to telling her that tomorrow I'd be living somewhere else, without Jamie, without Rhianna and I wouldn't see her or Matt again for ages. I don't know how I did it really. Old Mackintosh, my drama teacher, should put me up for the lead role in the school play. Except I won't be at the same school. I'll be at yet another new place with no friends because I can't get into anyone's stupid little clique and I'll be spending every break-time head down, walking purposefully round pretending I'm just on my way to meet up with my fantastic gang of super cool mates.

Hopeless. It was all totally hopeless.

Chapter 5

Mrs Frankish cooked us tea because the hospital phoned Paul. He looked really scared and when I asked, he said he had to rush up there to take Sarah a fresh nightie. She'd only been there one day! It must be a really posh hospital and if you spill your dinner or something you have to change your nightie or they shout at you and tell you off. When Mum was in hospital they never told her off and she used to knock things over all the time.

There was this lady there and she used to come and do Mum's lovely long hair every week until it went all thin and wispy and then she'd only let me do it. I'd bring in all my hair slides and scrunchees and lay them on the bed cover and she'd pick which ones she wanted. Then I'd put them in really gently and bring the little mirror over and show her and it would make her smile for a little while.

I didn't have time to finish my card for Sarah. It says *GET WE*. After Paul rushed off I went into the kitchen and told Mrs Frankish he had forgotten to take the clean nightie with him and Sarah would get into big trouble. She said couldn't I see she was busy cooking tea and told me to go away and not to be so silly. She had three blobs of orange sploppy stuff on her black jacket. They looked like three orange ladybirds.

Tea was yucky. It was supposed to be spaghetti hoops with little sausages but because she's a witch I think she bunged in some chopped worms or frogs' eyeballs when no one was looking. Jamie ate mine. Do you know, he said he really liked it! Vicky said she was a vegetibblarian and made herself a ham sandwich when Mrs Frankish was on the phone. Then Vicky and me got the birthday cake out of the box and put the candles on it. I blew them all out twice and made two wishes but I can't tell you what I wished for because if I do they won't come true. Sorry. I had three and a half pieces of cake because Vicky left most of hers.

After tea we went out into the garden to Jamie's tree house. He didn't usually let us in but he said we could come up as long as we didn't touch anything. Vicky told him she wouldn't want to touch his scrotty old rubbish but she came anyway to get away from Mrs Frankish.

I loved Jamie's tree house, it was like a little wooden nest but instead of soft feathers to line it, he'd pinned up all the postcards from Dad. He's a lorry driver and when he used to drive somewhere he would always post Jamie a card. He's got millions and billions and trillions. I tried to count them once but I kept getting it wrong. It's a good job Dad doesn't send them any more because there isn't any space left.

Once at school Jamie told this boy Ollie Stanmore about them all but Ollie didn't believe him so Jamie whacked him. Jamie does a lot of whacking. I heard Mrs Frankish tell Sarah that it's because he's got a lot of emotional baggage but that's not true he's only got his school rucksack. (Mrs Frankish gave him five bin liners for all his stuff!) Sarah and Paul had to go and see Mr Biggs and Mrs Featherstone because Jamie gave Ollie a nosebleed once and he nearly got secluded from school. Jamie said he didn't care and it served him right but then Mrs Featherstone asked what would your Dad say if he knew what you'd done, and he started crying. He never cries. Once he fell off the climbing frame in the park and broke his arm but he didn't even cry then and the bone was all poking out and there was blood everywhere.

I tried to count all the postcards again. I got to twenty-seven but then I gave up because I couldn't concentrate. I wished Dad was still living with us. Every Friday night when he came back from work, he used to bring me a big tube of Smarties. He'd watch me line them up on the table in their different colours and then I'd count them and do some sums before I ate them. He always helped me get the answers right. Sometimes, when he used to come home late, Mum would let us wait up for him. He'd come through the front door and we'd run up to him in a mad bundle. He was the strongest man in the whole world. He could pick us all up in one go and swing us round and

Mum would laugh and yell at him to watch the ornaments. Sometimes when I try to talk to Vicky about Mum and Dad she says there's no point remembering anything because it's like watching someone else's home movie. I don't know what she means and she gets all cross if I ask.

Vicky was in a real moody in the tree house. Manky Matt was coming round later and Mrs Frankish had said she couldn't go out. She had to pack all her stuff. I didn't think I wanted to go to this new school any more. Not without Vicky and Jamie. We were all sitting around on the mouldy cushions when Jamie told us his Big Idea. He said we should run away because then they couldn't split us up. I looked over at Vicky. She was biting her nails like they were really itching her or something.

I said, 'Can we run away to Disneyland?'

'We'll go somewhere better,' said Jamie.

I looked at Vicky again. 'What about it?'

'What about what!?' She sounded really snappy.

'Running away.'

'They're only going to split us up for a while – when the baby's born they'll have us back.'

Vicky got up but Jamie tugged at her arm. 'What if they don't?' he said.

'They've promised.'

'But what if something happens or they change their minds?'

Vicky pulled a face then stared out of the little tree house doorway. 'It's a stupid idea; we've got nowhere to go.'

'We could go to my secret camp in the woods,' said

Jamie picking up one of the postcards from the floor. 'Just for a bit. Until everything's all right again. It would be like when we went on holiday with Mum and Dad to Great Auntie Irene's.'

We've only been to Great Auntie Irene's once. Vicky, Jamie, Dad and me camped out in a tent on a little island in the middle of this big lake.

Mum slept in the house with Great Auntie Irene because she was cold all the time. Great Auntie Irene's dog Jip came with us and we all got in the rowing boat and rowed out to the island. We made a campfire and cooked potatoes in foil and marshmallows on sticks. The potatoes were all black on the outside and hard on the inside. Mum wasn't going to let us eat them – she said we'd be ill. But we did and we weren't. She was the one that kept being sick. She never even ate any potato. She did have a tiny nibble on my marshmallow but that was all. She didn't really want it but I said, 'Go on Mum, you've got to have a taste.'

Maxine can't eat peanuts, she's mlergic to them. If she has just one tiny weeny bit of peanut she'll puff up like a balloon and be really ill. It's true. Mrs Edwards told me. Maybe that's why Mum isn't here any more. Maybe she was mlergic to marshmallows. She didn't puff up, she just slowly shrank thinner and thinner until one day she disappeared and wasn't at the hospital any more. Maybe that tiny little bit I gave her was what started it all. She must be better by now. I just wish she'd hurry up and come home because I want to show her my new Furby.

Jamie was explaining to Vicky about his camp and how no one knew about it. I told Vicky about the ferny little den and the campfire but she just pulled a face and told us to forget it. She got up and started climbing down the ladder when Jamie stopped her.

'We've got to stay together Vick,' he said in a whisper. 'What's going to happen to Re if we're not around?'

'I don't need Miss Sticky Slob Bottom, thank you very much,' I said but the words came out all wobbly.

'We could look after ourselves,' Jamie pleaded but then Vicky said all snappy, 'Oh yeah? Great idea – just like last time.'

'That wasn't my fault!' Jamie called after her but Vicky didn't stop, she just ran up the garden into the house and slammed the back door behind her.

'It wasn't my fault Re,' said Jamie when she'd gone. 'I didn't want them to take us away from Dad.'

I remember when it happened. It was a long time ago. It was after Mum had gone. We'd all got in from school and Dad was out driving a lorry for Mr McCready. Mr McCready was so funny. When he came round to give Dad his money he'd always look round first like his mum was going to pop out of the bushes and tell him off for doing something naughty. Anyway that evening Jamie said he was fed up with jam sandwiches because Dad was never there to cook tea so he said he would make us all chips. Bossy old Vicky told him not to but he didn't take any notice. I love chips especially with loads of ketchup. He put the oil in the pan and turned the cooker on and then there was this cartoon on telly so we went and watched it for a while.

When we came back in the kitchen it was full of smoke. I called Vicky and she shouted at Jamie to come out and shut the door. Vicky had to go next door and get Mrs Cantoni to call 999. Everyone in the street came out when the fire engine arrived. A bit later Mrs Frankish turned up with a police lady and said we had to go with them.

When Dad came to see us in the first children's home he looked different. His face was all rough and scratchy when I gave him a kiss. Jamie told him a joke. Jamie said it was really funny but Dad never even laughed, he just sort of twisted his mouth up like he had a pain somewhere. When Jamie said, 'Your turn,' Dad said he'd run out of jokes at the moment. He didn't even smell like Dad any more. He smelt of beer and Jamie's PE kit when it needs a good wash.

Chapter 6

It was starting to get dark when Mrs Frankish went out to the tree house. I was in my bedroom waiting for Matt to arrive. OK so Cowpat-face wasn't going to let me go out but she couldn't stop Matt coming round to see me. I could hear Jamie shouting at her that she was an old bat and old bats weren't allowed in. Terrific. Matt was bound to turn up right in the middle of my embarrassing brother and my embarrassing sister screaming and yelling at my embarrassing social worker. What more could a girl want?

Mind you, nothing phases our Mrs Frankish. She just waited for a gap in between Rhianna's yells and Jamie's abuse, then called up that Paul was home and they both had to go in and pack their stuff ready for tomorrow. Rhianna pretended she couldn't hear her but of course old

Frankenstein wasn't having it. She just gave her that look that she does. She takes a great big breath, makes her eyes go all slitty and looks down her nose at you like she's going to turn you into something scrungy. No wonder Rhianna's convinced she's a witch. Jamie once told Rhianna that she's got a whole load of boxes in the boot of her car. He said one day, when Mrs Frankish was talking to Paul, he sneaked out and opened one. Inside there was a frog hopping around and it was still wearing a little school uniform. He might be an annoying little brat but he sure has got one hell of an imagination. Ever since then Rhianna's never played her up for long.

I went downstairs and saw Paul sitting in the kitchen. Rhianna was asking him if Sarah liked her card but he just looked at her as if he'd forgotten who she was or something. It was that same look Dad had the week before Mum died. He'd come home from the hospital and just sit in a chair for hours, staring at the wall like he'd been turned to stone or something. Then suddenly he'd start talking about all the mad, crazy things we were all going to do together when Mum got better and came home. About two days before she died, Dad was going on and on about how we'd all have a fantastic holiday together next summer. I couldn't stand it any longer. I yelled at him, 'For goodness' sake, Mum isn't going to get better – she's going to die!' The minute the words were out I wished I hadn't said them. But it was too late. He just looked at me for a few seconds then the tears started rolling down his cheeks and he started sobbing really loudly. I didn't know what to do. He was supposed to be the grown-up, not me.

Mrs Frankish made Paul a cup of tea and started spooning sugar in. Rhianna told her he didn't like sugar but Mrs Frankish kept on shovelling it in like it was suddenly going to make everything all right.

'I'll help you pack all your things, Rhianna,' she said with a big, bright smile pasted over her face. 'Paul just needs to have a few quiet minutes on his own.'

'He still won't drink your stinky tea,' Rhianna retorted.

They went upstairs and Jamie followed. I looked at Paul. I don't think he even realised I was there. I was scared to ask about Sarah. I was even more scared to ask about the baby. So I turned and walked out of the kitchen door into the garden and took a big gulp of air. I staggered to the garden wall and sat down, feeling sick. I sat there for a while just trying to get my head together. Then I saw Matt coming along the road. It was too late to go in, he'd already seen me and gave a wave. I didn't want him to see me like this. I knew I looked a real sight.

'Hey,' I said, trying to sound as casual as I could.

'Hi, gorgeous.'

No one's ever, ever called me gorgeous before. He put his arm round me and drew me close to him. He was actually going to kiss me! My first proper kiss! I know it was wrong, with Sarah and the baby and everything but for a few perfect seconds I just felt so happy. Wait till I tell Rosie, I thought. Stuff Romeo and Juliet. This was the real thing. Our lips were just touching – eat your heart out Charlene Slackton – and I was melting in his arms . . . when suddenly I heard a yell from our bedroom window and I felt something land on my head.

It was a pair of her pants! Can you believe it! A pair of Rhianna's manky, navy-blue school pants! The cow! I'll kill her! I thought. I will personally kill her!

Matt laughed and called up to her but I was furious. How dare she! How dare she ruin my first kiss! Possibly the only kiss I was going to get for the next century as I was banished into the unknown. Something in me flipped and I started yelling at her. I saw Matt look a bit taken aback but I didn't stop. Now *I* was the embarrassing one for a change. It was like everything had bubbled up into one big gigantic mess and I couldn't keep the lid on it all any more.

I haven't thrown a real full-blown wobbly since I was about eight but this definitely made up for it. Mrs Frankish came out in a flurry.

'This is all your fault!' I screamed, throwing the pants at her. 'If you hadn't taken us away from Dad in the first place, we wouldn't be in this mess, packing up to go God knows where!'

She tried to say something but I wouldn't let her, so she just stood there holding the pants and going more and more red as I heard myself screeching at her more and more loudly. The nosy woman from over the road came out to have a look but I still didn't stop yelling. I couldn't stop if I wanted to. And what's more, I didn't want to. Everything I cared about was going to be taken away from me. I'd got nothing to lose. I was going to yell like crazy – scream like a loony. I was going to get my money's worth. Matt started to fidget then he mumbled some excuse and said he had better get going.

'Matt,' I said, 'don't go!' But he just gave me a wary sort of smile then walked off down the road and out of my life. Watching him hurry away slowed me down. Suddenly I was drained. I'd got nothing left to say. He turned the corner and I burst into tears just as Paul came out. I heard him quietly say to Mrs Frankish that he'd manage now and she'd better get off too. She didn't look too happy but Paul insisted. She told him she'd be round the next morning to collect us. She patted his arm and then, still holding the pair of pants, got in her car and drove off. I looked down and saw I was shaking. It was really weird – I was shaking like a jelly and I couldn't stop. Paul turned to me.

'Come on, love,' he said gently. 'Let's get you inside. It's cold out here.'

Chapter 7

I ran into Jamie's room to hide from Vicky. I could hear her outside screaming. I didn't mean to make her that angry. I hid under Jamie's bed and put my fingers in my ears. I wanted the noise to stop but it didn't so I started screaming too. Jamie came in. He bent down and put his face under the bed.

'Stop it Re!' he called. 'Stop that racket right now . . . or I'll give you a double chinese burn.'

He does really nasty chinese burns so I stopped.

'That's better,' he said as he got out his school rucksack. 'Right, well come on then, get out from under there.'

I crawled out from under the bed covered in dust.

He opened his school bag and looked at me. 'Now watch carefully because you'll have to pack your rucksack too in a minute.'

'What about the suitcase Paul gave you?' I asked.

'People don't carry suitcases around when they're running away. They need to travel light,' he said. 'With just the things they *really* need.'

'Are we really going to run away?' I asked.

'It'll be fun.'

I thought for a second. 'What about Vicky?'

'Vicky's a big fat pain in the bum. All she cares about is her stupid boyfriend.'

'Manky Matt.'

'Yeah. Manky old Matt. We don't need her bossing us around all the time.'

'No we don't.'

Jamie put in his warm jumper, some jeans, two pairs of thick socks, his torch, his spiderman sleeping bag and his camping book.

'Right,' he said, 'now go and pack yours just with stuff you really need.'

'OK,' I said and ran quickly off to our bedroom.

I got out my school rucksack and piled in my Furby, my baldy Barbies, my disco lamp and Baby Emma with the poked out eyes. Last of all I put in the big photo of me, Vicky, Jamie and Mum and Dad. Great Auntie Irene had taken it outside her house. She was really really old and had cracks on her face like dried up playdough. The photo was a bit blurry. It looked like it was raining but it wasn't, it was lovely and sunny. Vicky's got her eyes shut because she blinked and you can hardly see Jamie because he crouched down behind Jip to keep him still.

Jamie came in. 'You'll have to sleep in your jumper and jeans tonight,' he said as he helped me roll up my sleeping bag and fix it on top. 'And we have to do a secret commando raid to get some food and our drinks bottles.'

He told me to go down and talk to Paul in the sitting room while he sneaked into the kitchen.

'What shall I talk about?' I asked.

'Doesn't matter. Anything will do.'

In the sitting room Paul was talking to Vicky. She wasn't yelling any more, just making funny sort of gulps every now and then. Paul gave her a tissue and she blew her nose.

'How long will we have to be away?' Vicky asked Paul.

'I don't know,' he said.

'It'll only be a short while though, won't it?'

Paul still didn't say anything.

'We'll be back before Christmas, definitely. We will be back then.'

Paul didn't answer.

Vicky looked at him. 'Promise me we will.'

'I'm sorry Vicky . . . things change – I can't say because I just don't know.'

Vicky made a funny snorty noise then rushed upstairs saying she was going to pack her stuff.

I love Christmas. Vicky and Jamie don't believe in Father Christmas but I do. And I know how he gets down chimneys too. You know he's really fat? Ha! Well, he isn't actually. All that fatness is just air. When he wants to

32

come down a chimney he just pulls at a string on his belly button and all the air whooshes out from his tummy and he goes really skinny. That's how he can slip down the chimney. Then, when he gets to the bottom and he's left all the presents, he pulls another string and blows himself up again like a balloon.

When we were little, Dad used to bring us presents when he came back from driving. Mum would get cross sometimes and tell him she needed the money to pay the bills but he would just laugh and say they could whistle for it. After Mum was gone, two men came round to take our beds and the sofa and armchairs back to the shop but they didn't whistle. One was really grumpy and the other just kept saying he didn't want any trouble. When they'd gone Dad said not to worry because every cloud had a silver lining. I looked outside to see but they were all grey. Anyway he'd found some money under the sofa so he took us out to get chips for tea. We had cola and he had some beer. We came back and sat on the carpet with the chips on the paper in the middle like a big picnic. It was fun. Mum never let us do stuff like that. And he never got cross when I spilt my cola. He just said it didn't matter any more because they'd be back for the carpet next week.

I heard Jamie in the kitchen banging about. Paul heard him too.

'Paul,' I said quickly, 'do you want to hear a joke?'

He looked round me at the kitchen door.

'It's the funniest joke ever, in the whole wide world,' I said.

'Go on then,' he said. I looked at him. His eyes were really red and tired. Suddenly I wanted to cheer him up. I really really did want to tell him the funniest joke ever in the whole wide world but I didn't know how. You see I don't actually know any jokes at all. Jamie tells me them all the time but I get all mixed up and can never remember them.

It was a good job that the next second Jamie came out of the kitchen. He gave me a thumbs-up sign and ran upstairs with a bag.

'Gotta go,' I said running out and following Jamie upstairs.

'Thought you were going to tell me the funniest joke in the whole wide world?' said Paul, calling after me.

'Nah,' I said. 'It's really boring.'

chapter 8

I went to bed early that night. I'd packed my stuff and didn't feel like going back downstairs. Mainly I was kind of embarrassed about my whopping great tantrum earlier. I couldn't believe how I just lost the plot so completely. In front of Matt too. Errrch! I couldn't bear to think of it, but Matt's bewildered and wary expression kept flashing up in my mind's eye. He probably thought I was a right head-case. A complete nutter. Maybe it's a good thing we're leaving tomorrow, I thought. At least I wouldn't have to face him at school for a while.

Paul had been on tenterhooks all evening in case the hospital rang but no one did, thank goodness. He phoned at nine and the ward sister said Sarah was comfortable, whatever that meant. Poor Sarah. She and Paul so wanted this baby. We all did. Rhianna and Jamie had already gone to bed. I guess they were as fed up as me. At least Re got her Furby and her cake. I looked over at her, snuggled up under the covers and fast asleep, an old teddy bear tucked in next to her. There was the faintest trace of a smile on her large moon face; she looked like she hadn't a care in the world. The great thing about Re was she never stayed miserable for long. She lived in the present and never beat herself up over things she should have done or didn't do – they were in the past and they just didn't matter any more. And she never really worried about what was going to happen. She lived for the moment. That was all. Boy was she lucky. When Mum died, I tried to soften it all for her. There I was launching into this big 'Mum's gone but everything's going to be all right' routine and when I finished she just looked at me with those big grey eyes and asked if we could have pot noodle for tea.

I'd been furious with her earlier but being angry with Re is like being angry with a puppy that's chewed one of your best trainers. Just one look at its trusting, dopey expression and you can't help but forgive it. Maybe this residential school wouldn't be so bad. And maybe, if I was with a decent family, they'd take me to visit or even let Re stay at the weekend. Maybe Sarah would get better really quickly and we'd all be back together for when the baby arrived . . . maybe everything would work out perfectly . . . maybe little pink pigs would learn to fly and take over the world . . . Maybe. I was sick of maybes. Paul had said he didn't know when we would be coming back. 'Things change.' What exactly did he mean?

A really horrible thought rushed into my head and no matter how hard I tried, I couldn't push it out. What if 'I don't know' became 'Never'? Jamie was right. We'd be split up for good and powerless to do anything about it. I told myself to shut up. Sarah and Paul wouldn't let us down. They wouldn't. They cared about us. Wanted the best for us. But then, we had been let down so many times over the last two years. Promises, like balloons, had popped in front of our eyes. Mrs Frankish was always saying that things are never as bad as you imagine. But it's all right for her, she has the imagination of a fruit fly.

Chapter 9

When I woke up, Jamie was standing over me with his finger on his lips.

'It's time to go Re,' he whispered.

I looked over at Vicky. She was curled up asleep in her bed. I didn't feel like going anywhere but Jamie picked up my school rucksack and we tiptoed out so she wouldn't wake up. We crept down the stairs in the dark. The house was fast asleep. I couldn't see where I was going so I grabbed Jamie's arm. I tripped over Vicky's shoes in the hall and banged my knee on the little telephone table. It hurt so bad I wanted to cry but Jamie put his hand over my mouth to stop me. We put on our trainers and coats. Then really quietly he undid the front door.

Out in the street it was quiet and still. The black cat from next door came up to us and rubbed his back round my legs. I gave him a quick stroke and he stared at us as we disappeared off down the street. I bet he wondered where we were going. A car came up the road so we hid behind the letterbox but the man driving never saw us. Nobody did.

When we got near the woods everything was even darker so Jamie said he would switch on his torch to light the way. I don't think it was working properly because it only made a little tiny circle of yellow on the pavement.

'It'll warm up,' Jamie said, but it didn't.

I don't like the dark. When we first went to Paul and Sarah's they said we could each have our own room but I didn't like the shadows that came at night-time so I used to creep into Vicky's bed and snuggle up next to her. She'd give me a hug and stroke my hair. If I shut my eyes tight sometimes I could pretend it was Mum back home. In the end Sarah said that we'd better move my bed in and share the room so Vicky could get some sleep. Now my old room is painted ready for the baby and there are lovely new curtains with rabbits and ducks on them but I don't care, I'd rather be with Vicky.

The path down into the woods looked like a big black mouth.

'I don't like it,' I told Jamie, 'I'm not going down there.'

'It'll be OK. Anyway we'll be at the camp soon.'

I wouldn't budge so he got cross.

'We can't go back now Re!' he said, taking my arm and trying to pull me in.

I was stronger than him. He couldn't make me so in the

end he started walking down the path into the woods on his own. I watched him go and then looked around. I didn't know which way to go. I wanted Vicky. She always knew what to do. Suddenly I heard a really scary noise. The shadow things were coming to get me now I was on my own. They'd waited for Jamie to go off and now they saw their chance. I screamed then ran after Jamie as fast as I could.

When I caught up with him, he told me to stop bawling my head off or he'd whack me and then I would have something to cry about.

'But I'm scared of the monsters!'

He laughed. 'I'm not! If any monsters try anything I'll just give them a karate kick in their rudey bits then finish them off by thumping them one.'

Jamie's really brave. I'd just run away if there was a monster standing in front of me ready to pull my arms and legs off or suck out my blood.

It started to spit with rain but Jamie said it didn't matter because when we got to his camp we'd crawl inside his den and be warm and dry like two snug bugs in a rug. He got out two penguin bars that he'd pinched from the biscuit tin. He let me have the one with the red wrapper. The red ones taste the best. He said we'd have a competition to see who could make theirs last the longest. I won by loads.

I'd just finished the last little crumb when we got to the camp. It looked different in the dark. Some of the branches of the den had caved in and some had blown away. He said he'd mend it and he started pulling them all off and piling them up on the roof again. It took him ages and he kept swearing when they fell off. When he'd done it we got out our sleeping bags, unrolled them on the floor of the den and crawled inside.

'I can smell dog wee,' I said.

'Shut up Re.'

It was like lying on prickly hedgehogs and my hands still felt cold. Jamie said he'd blow on them to warm them up. He made a funny 'hhrrrrr' noise like a dragon blowing out smoke. Ollie Stanmore nicks fags from his dad and he can blow smoke rings. He showed Jamie how to do it once but Jamie just took a couple of puffs and started coughing. Smoking is bad for you. Mrs Edwards told us that in our Healthy Bodies lesson. We watched a video of some lungs filling up with black stuff just like Marmite and a voice said 'smoking kills' really loudly. I kept telling Dad that after Mum had gone but he said he needed them to go with his beer. I said, don't have your beer then but he said he needed it to go with his fags. I said his lungs would fill up with Marmite and then he'd get really ill but he told me not to worry.

The good thing was that he did stop soon after that. He went off beer and just had a bottle of whisky every night instead. Sometimes Maxine lets me have some of her break-time drink from her bottle so I let her have some of mine. It's nice to have a change. Dad drank the whole bottle really quickly and didn't even bother about having a smoke. So that was OK. Jamie tried some once. Dad had fallen asleep when we were all watching Pet Rescue on the telly and

Jamie tried the last drops at the bottom of the bottle. He said it tasted like cough medicine but worse. I love cough medicine. Especially cherry flavour. Jamie was a right meanie, he didn't leave any for me to try.

I was just falling asleep when Jamie jabbed me with his elbow. 'Stop taking up all the room!' he hissed.

'I'm not taking up all the room!'

'You are, you fat lump!'

'I am not fat! Don't call me fat because I'm not fat!'

'Move over!'

He started pushing me. I pushed him back so he gave me a whopping great shove right in my side.

'Stop it you conkhog!' I yelled. He shoved me again. Harder. I rolled into the wall. Some of the branches fell down on my head. Jamie started going balloony.

'You're trashing my den!'

'It's a rubbish den!' I yelled back at him. 'You said we'd be as snug as bugs in a rug!'

Then we heard the noise outside.

'It's the monsters Jamie!'

'Shush!'

'With stabby beaks.'

'Shut up Re!'

'They can stab their way through branches.'

'Rhianna! Put a cork in it!'

'You've got to do something!'

But Jamie didn't get up. He just wriggled down in his sleeping bag till I could only see the top of his hair. Then he said in a funny wobbly voice that he wasn't going anywhere.

'But you said you'd do karate kicks if any monsters came. You promised!'

'Will you shut up!' He sounded really cross. I told him it wasn't my fault the monsters were outside waiting to bite off our heads. Jamie hissed if I didn't shut up straight away he'd bite off my head himself and save the monster the job of it. I started asking him how because he hasn't got pointy teeth but then we saw something coming towards us.

Jamie picked up one of the branches. He crawled out and started to wave it around his head. He didn't look very scary and his arm was shaking.

'Quick!' I screamed. 'Kick it in its rudey bits!'

Chapter 10

'Just you try it, Jamie Davies!' I shouted, flashing my torch at him. 'And put that stick down before you hurt yourself!'

'What are you doing here?' asked Jamie.

'I've come to take you home.'

'Oh yeah?' said Jamie. 'That'll be interesting. Seeing as we don't have a home at the moment.'

'Jamie and me have run away,' said Rhianna. 'And now you can too.'

'I'm not staying,' I said, avoiding Jamie's eye. 'You've both got to come back.'

'Why? Who's going to miss us?' he muttered. 'No one wants us now. Can't you see that, Vicky? We're just in the way, that's all. More paperwork for Mrs Frankish.'

'What about Dad?' I said.

'What about him?' asked Jamie, pulling a face.

I looked down at the ground and kicked at some leaves with my trainer.

'Maybe he wouldn't want you to run away,' I said awkwardly.

But Jamie wasn't listening any more. He'd turned round and walked back to the shelter.

'I'm not going and you can't make me,' he muttered as he crawled back inside.

I looked at Rhianna. 'Come on, Re. If we go back now we won't get in trouble. No one'll even know we've been out.' I took my hand in hers. It was freezing.

'OK,' she grinned. 'If you come to my new school with me.'

'I can't, Re. They won't let me.'

'I'm not going without you and Jamie.'

'It might not be that bad, Re. They've got a pool. You love swimming. And you'd make lots of new friends and it won't be for ever . . .' My voice went all funny. Like I was fighting with the words and they were winning. I stopped and turned away.

'What's the matter?'

'Nothing,' I snapped, 'I've got something in my eye. That's all.'

I couldn't do it. I couldn't pretend any more that when we were split up it was only going to be for a while. It was all a big fat porky and I knew it. I'd known it when I'd packed my rucksack (just in case) and followed Jamie and Rhianna out the front door and down to the woods. Deep down I knew I wouldn't be coming back. Jamie was right.

We weren't wanted. I just hadn't wanted to admit it. Not out loud.

When we first went to school, the authorities thought Re could manage without any help but every morning at the school gate Mum would whisper to me, 'Keep an eye on your sister, Vicky.' So I did. I looked out for her. Kept the bad kids away. Protected her from danger. Every single day. And now Mum was dead I would always have to look out for her. For ever and ever. Amen. I took a deep breath.

'So let's see this fantastic den,' I said quietly, a few seconds later. With a big grin on her face, Rhianna took me over to the entrance and pulled me in. It looked a bit of a mess. Ten to one it was chock full of creepy crawlies too. Ugh! I hate things like that. I took my rucksack off my back and pulled out my sleeping bag.

'I thought you wanted to go "home",' said Jamie in his 'I won, so there' voice.

'I'm not leaving you two here on your own,' I said, unrolling my sleeping bag and laying it next to Rhianna's. 'Anything could happen.'

Chapter 11

When I woke up everything was green. It was like being in the Emerald City in The Wizard of Oz except it was cold and the top of my sleeping bag was all damp. I bet Dorothy didn't have a soggy sleeping bag. I bet hers was all nice and cosy and warm. Something tickly was crawling in my hair and I could hear Jamie and Vicky laughing somewhere. Then I remembered. I wasn't in the Emerald City, I was in Jamie's little den in the woods. We'd really done it. We'd really run away together. I wriggled out of my sleeping bag and crawled outside.

'Welcome to Camp Fun,' said Jamie in a funny posh voice when he saw me. 'And would modom care for some breakfast? I'm afraid we're all out of cereal.'

'Good!' I said. 'Cereal is pantyhose.'

'But we do have a bag of the finest jam doughnuts.'

He brushed some mud off the bag and opened it. Yippeee! I love doughnuts. Things were getting better and better. (I bet Dorothy didn't have jam doughnuts.) I put my hand in and pulled out a lovely, squishy, jammy blob.

'There's two and a bit each,' said Vicky, pulling out another one. 'And there's milk to drink.' She sniffed the carton then took a big swig. Milk dribbled down her chin.

'Vicky you mucky mess pup!' I laughed.

'Who cares?' said Jamie. 'This is *our* camp. We can do what we like. There's no rules, no adults to boss us around and no worries!'

'No worries! No worries! We've got no worries!' I grabbed Vicky's arm and we danced round and round, laughing and giggling.

Suddenly we heard a noise. Someone was coming. Vicky quickly pushed me back into the den and dived in after me.

'Don't make a sound!' she hissed in my ear.

Jamie pushed his way in and we sat there all in a tumble like we were playing musical bumps. Vicky had trodden on my foot and it was hurting like mad. What if it was Mrs Frankish? She would be so cross she'd turn us all into frogs. I didn't want to be a frog. I hate frogs. This wasn't how running away was supposed to be. Jamie said we weren't going to have any worries. I started crying and Vicky put her hand over my mouth. We listened for a few seconds. Someone was outside walking around. A face appeared at the little doorway.

Vicky and I screamed but Jamie laughed. It was his friend Sam.

'I was going to knock for you, like we said yesterday, but they're going barmy back at your house. There's a police car and everything.'

'A police car! Great!' said Jamie.

'It is not great,' snapped Vicky, 'It's awful. Think what Paul must be going through.'

'What's going on?' Sam asked.

'Sarah's in hospital,' Vicky told him. 'They can't foster us any more. We were going to be split up so we came here.'

'I'm not going back,' said Jamie.

'I know,' I said, 'maybe we could phone Paul up on Vicky's mobile and tell him we're OK but we've just run away.'

'Great idea,' said Jamie. 'The minute we do that, they'll find us.'

'They'll soon find you anyway,' said Sam. 'They're going to do a search – I heard the policeman telling some woman.'

'Mrs Frankish,' said Vicky.

'She's really a witch Sam,' I said. Someone had to tell him.

'Oh yeah?'

'Yeah. She'll probably get her broomstick out and fly overhead like in The Wizard of Oz,' I said, feeling all shivery.

'Don't you worry Rhianna – we'll just chuck a load of water over her and she'll melt into a trail of green slime.'

'Thanks Sam.' I liked him.

Vicky looked up. 'We can't stay here. We've got to go somewhere where they won't be able to find us. Somewhere a long way away. Somewhere we'll be safe.'

'Where's that?' I asked.

'I don't know, but if we don't get going right now, we won't have a chance.'

She started stuffing things back in my rucksack. 'Rhianna what the hell is all this?' she exclaimed suddenly, pulling out one of my baldy Barbies.

'Jamie told me to take all the things I needed. So I did.'

'I give up,' sighed Vicky, bundling the rest of my stuff out of the rucksack.

'Watch my Furby!'

She grabbed the photo Great Auntie Irene had taken. Jamie looked at it.

'That's it!' he shouted. 'We'll go and stay at Great Auntie Irene's.'

'But she's really old,' said Vicky.

'So? We can help her with chores and things she can't do any more . . . Carry heavy shopping and take Jip for long walks for her. It's perfect!'

'How are we going to get there Jamie?' asked Vicky. 'She lives miles away out in the country. Don't you remember the journey there, with you throwing up all the time and Rhianna asking if we were nearly there so many times that she drove Dad bonkers. Anyway, how much money have you got?'

'Twenty pence.'

'Rhianna?'

'Nothing.'

Vicky put her hand in her pocket and bought out some money. 'Forty pounds. Our birthday money. That won't get us far.'

'I've got an idea,' said Jamie, stuffing his sleeping bag back in his rucksack. 'Get your things together. We've got to hurry.'

Sam helped me bundle all my stuff back in my rucksack but Vicky was getting cross because Jamie wouldn't tell us where we were going. When we were all ready he just said, 'Follow me!' and charged off at a hundred miles an hour.

chapter 12

'Jamie! Sam! Slow down. Wait for us!' I didn't like to yell in case someone heard us, but it was still early and luckily we didn't meet anyone. Jamie led us out of the woods along the footpath by the gas works and up the back roads to Mr McCready's depot. There were a few lorries parked inside the tatty yard, which was edged with rusty iron railings.

We watched from behind a scrubby bush. The place was pretty quiet. Too early for McCready, the old crook. It was partly his fault about Dad. He was always getting him to drop off his dodgy stuff. Maybe Dad didn't realise that it was all stolen, I thought suddenly. Maybe Dad was completely innocent and had just ended up being the fall guy . . . Huh. Who was I kidding? Dad knew full well what he was doing.

There were a couple of drivers in the portakabin having

a brew before they set off on their journeys. I could see them inside, laughing and chatting and swigging their tea. I recognised one of them. It was Pete, one of Dad's old mates from years back. He was all right, was Pete. Used to give us wine gums. He carried round bumper packs of them because he was trying to give up smoking, but he just got addicted to them instead. Pete always used to do the same trip up north, covering the same territory and always dropping in to see his 'old Mum' on the way. Then I clicked. I understood Jamie's plan. Pete's mum lived about thirty miles away from Great Auntie Irene – one year Pete had even made a detour to her house to deliver some Christmas presents from us.

If we could just get on to his lorry he'd unknowingly take us most of the way for free. Perfect. I grinned at Jamie who was looking pretty pleased with himself.

'Not bad, you little tyke,' I said. 'Come on.'

Carefully we climbed up and over the railings into the yard, then scuttled towards the parked lorries. But which one was Pete's? I hadn't got a clue. If we got on the wrong one it would be a disaster. We could end up anywhere. Suddenly Rhianna started jumping up and down excitedly.

'Shut up, Rhianna!' I hissed at her.

'It's this one!' she said, pointing to a red lorry with a battered knitted teddy bear tied to the grill at the front. 'Remember?' she asked. 'Pete told me his name's Lucky.'

Inside the cab on the dashboard we found three full packets of wine gums and the debris of several others. Rhianna was right. This was definitely Pete's lorry.

As quickly and quietly as we could, we went round the back. Pete's teddy bear was bringing us luck too – the doors were unlocked. We scrambled in and said our goodbyes to Sam. Jamie made him swear he wouldn't tell anyone where we were going. He promised and closed the doors after us. We groped our way forward in the semi-dark, sat ourselves down behind some cardboard crates and waited.

About ten minutes later we heard the doors being rattled and locked and then the sound of Pete getting into his cab. We heard him start up the engine and then felt a sudden lurch forward as the lorry pulled out of the depot.

We'd done it. We were on our way. Jamie gave me a thumbs-up and I grinned back at him. We were together, the three of us, and everything was going to be all right.

We got out our sleeping bags and quietly made ourselves as comfortable as possible. I was petrified Pete might hear us so we sat in silence to start with, huddled together, listening to the drone of the lorry's engine. After a while we became a bit more confident and started talking in whispers about all the things we were going to do when we got to Great Auntie Irene's. A couple of hours passed and the journey dragged on. We were quiet now. And tired. Jamie and Rhianna fell asleep, one after the other, which was probably a good thing as they wouldn't feel sick. About another two hours later I was just beginning to doze off when I felt the lorry pull to a halt. Maybe we're at Pete's mum's, I thought.

Quickly, I woke Rhianna and Jamie and we hid behind some of the boxes. We waited, hardly daring to breathe as we heard the doors at the back of the lorry open. From behind the boxes we could hear Pete rearranging some of the crates near the doors. I looked over at Jamie and saw to my horror he was pulling really strange faces. What on earth was he playing at? Now wasn't the time for silly games. Suddenly I realised. He was trying to stop himself sneezing.

All at once he let out an enormous 'Ahhhh-tishooo!'

'Who's in there?' Pete called out roughly. 'Come on – show yourself. Get out of there now!'

There was nothing for it. We all stood up.

'Pete?' I called. 'It's only us. Neil Davies's kids.'

'Neil's kids?' He lowered the crowbar he was holding. 'Vicky, isn't it?'

'Yeah. It's me and Rhianna and Jamie.'

'What are you all doing in my lorry?'

'Running away,' Rhianna chipped in before I could stop her.

'Jamie, go and help Rhianna a minute,' I said as I quickly jumped down from the back of the lorry and pulled Pete to one side. I glanced round. We weren't at his mum's at all. We were in a huge car park full of lorries – part of a motorway service station.

'Pete,' I said. 'We need your help.'

'Where's your dad then? Haven't seen him for ages.'

'Working abroad,' I lied.

'Oh right.'

I could feel my cheeks burning. 'We're just going to stay with someone else for a bit. We needed a lift.'

'Sure,' said Pete quietly. 'Look, the lorry's full of apples.

Go and help yourself. I just need a break for five minutes or so then we'll get going.'

He walked to the cab and I dashed back to Rhianna.

'Where's Jamie?'

'Said he wanted to stretch his legs. Is Pete cross?'

'No. Everything's going to be fine,' I told her. 'We're going to be OK!'

She'd already got stuck into the apples. I told her to go easy or she'd end up with a bellyache. Just then Jamie appeared from round the other side of the lorry.

'Why's Pete talking about us?'

'What?' I asked.

'On his mobile.'

My stomach lurched.

'Quick!' I hissed. 'Get your stuff!'

We snatched up our bags. I looked round desperately. Which way? Beyond the car park, cars and lorries were roaring up and down the motorway. All around us were people, stretching their legs, sprawled out on the grass eating picnics and take-aways from boxes, exercising their dogs and taking a break from their journeys. The car park was fringed by a deserted stretch of scrubby woodland. Our only way out.

'Come on.' I grabbed one of Rhianna's hands and Jamie grabbed the other. Then . . . we ran. And ran.

Chapter 13

Vicky and Jamie pulled me along so hard my arms hurt. I yelled at them to stop but they wouldn't, even when I said I felt sick.

'You shouldn't have eaten all those apples Re,' said Vicky.

'I didn't eat them all, I only had five. There were boxes and boxes left.'

Vicky wouldn't tell me where we were going. I thought we were going to get back in Pete's lorry and ride in the front with him like I did once with Dad, but Vicky said we couldn't. She always spoils everything.

I was still feeling sick when we ran out of the wood and came to a road. I wanted to stop but Vicky said we had to keep going. But I didn't want to so I started crying. Vicky was shouting at me and Jamie was trying to pull me along when this car stopped. The lady driver wound down the window and asked if we were OK.

'Fine thank you,' Vicky told her. 'We're just going back home . . . um . . . we're a bit late. Our mum hates it when we're late.'

I looked at her. She was going bright red like a tomato.

The lady had short curly grey hair and nice orangey lipstick and she looked a bit like my teacher, Mrs Edwards. 'Well if you're sure . . .' She looked at us for a long time but then she drove off. We carried on but Vicky said we'd better not run any more in case people thought we were in trouble or had done something wrong. So we walked really quickly. It was just as bad. I asked Vicky if we could have spaghetti for dinner and cola to drink but she said no so I said what are we having then and she said she didn't know.

We came to a crossroads but Vicky didn't know the places on the road signs or which way to go. Jamie said we needed a map. Vicky told him they didn't grow on trees and that we'd have to find a shop or something. But we didn't even know which way to go to find a shop. Vicky decided we should go straight on for a bit because the other turnings were just lanes and she said there wouldn't be any shops down little lanes. So we went straight on along the main road for ages but she was wrong. We didn't see any shops at all.

Vicky got out the last doughnut and said if I carried on walking without making any fuss I could have it. I said OK. It was all squashed and the jam had squirted out. I gobbled it down in one gulp and I was still hungry.

We went up a hill and when we walked down the other side, we saw a petrol station by the side of the road.

'They might sell maps in there,' said Jamie.

'I'll go and find out,' said Vicky. 'Stay here, behind these bushes.'

I watched her walk into the petrol station shop.

'Keep your head down Re!' Jamie pulled me down behind the bush.

'Ow! You don't have to pull my arm!' I told him. I was cross. 'See how you like it.'

I pushed him and he fell back on to the ground.

Then Vicky came back. She looked cross.

'Rhianna! What are you doing?'

'He started it!'

'For goodness' sake!'

Jamie got up and gave me a bad look. A chinese burn look. I went and stood behind Vicky.

'All right. I've got a map. Now let's try and work out where we are.'

Vicky said we'd better keep away from the main roads just in case anyone was looking for us. She unfolded the map and looked at it for ages with Jamie. I asked her if we were nearly there and she said not far but we had to go all the way back to the crossroads then turn down one of the narrow lanes and walk a few miles until we got to the station. At the station we had to get on a train and when we got off the train we had to walk a bit more. I was tired and I didn't want to walk anywhere but going on a train was all right. That sounded like fun.

'Come on Re – if we keep going we'll soon be at Great Auntie Irene's,' said Jamie.

'Can we have spaghetti when we get there?'

'I expect so.'

'With cheese on top and no mushrooms in the sauce?'

Mushrooms are yucky.

'Course we can,' said Jamie. 'And we'll have a massive fry-up tomorrow – bacon, eggs and tomatoes and toast and jam and hot chocolate and muffins with chocolate chips. And Great Auntie Irene'll make us lovely dinners every single day . . . roast dinners too, like Mum used to.'

'With pudding afterwards?'

'And second helpings. Thirds if we want.'

Vicky laughed.

'We will!' said Jamie.

'Why not?' said Vicky with a shrug. 'Great Auntie Irene's a fantastic cook.'

'Can she make pizzas then?'

'With her arms tied behind her back juggling a squirrel on her nose,' said Jamie.

'Really?'

Jamie laughed. 'Course she'll be able to make pizzas Re. Don't worry.'

'And if she gets tired of cooking I can make cheese straws for her,' I said. 'I'm good at them.'

It was all going to be lovely. I couldn't wait. I started walking faster.

'Slow down Re!' called Vicky.

'No. You hurry up – I want to get there!'

Chapter 14

It was hard work keeping up with Re. For a start she's miles taller than Jamie and me and when she gets into her stride she really gets going. She wasn't moaning about being hungry any more – she was talking non-stop about all the fun we were going to have when we got to Great Auntie Irene's.

We reached the crossroads and turned left down the lane. I felt happier now, out of sight and away from the traffic of the main road. We tracked our way through the lanes following the map for about an hour before taking a right fork into the narrowest lane so far. Grass was growing through the tarmac down the middle and Rhianna and Jamie were playing a game jumping from clump to clump. About half an hour later, we rounded a bend and found ourselves at a dead end, standing in front of two huge wrought-iron gates. They were closed, blocking our route. The black paint was chipped off in places revealing patches of red rust like open wounds. Through the gates was a long tree-lined drive, dotted with crumbling, mossy statues on pedestals. On either side of the gates were high stone walls topped with spikes.

'What do we do now?' asked Jamie, climbing on one of the gates and swinging it forwards and back. It squeaked painfully.

'Get off there, Jamie.'

He carried on swinging. I checked the map then looked down the tree-lined drive.

'I don't understand it. The station's over that way. We must have taken a wrong turning somewhere.'

'I'm not going all the way back – it's miles and miles.'

'The drive comes out on the other side of the grounds. But we can't go that way – it's private.'

'Who says?' Jamie jumped off the gate and started walking down the pot-holed drive kicking the loose gravel as he went. 'Come on. It's our "private" short cut.'

I hesitated. To me those huge gates, high walls and sharp spikes were all shouting 'Keep out' pretty loudly. 'We better not.'

But Jamie wasn't listening and Re was already trotting after him down the drive. The pair of them were zigzagging from statue to statue, inspecting each one and sniggering at the more scantily dressed ones.

I looked round. Everything was so neglected I wondered if anyone even lived there any more.

'Hey, Vicky, this one's "armless"!' Jamie was standing behind the stone torso of a woman, waving his arms around as Re giggled uncontrollably.

I weighed up the risk. If we just nipped through and out the other side, likely as not no one would see us – no one would even know we'd been there. On the other hand, if we went back all the way we'd come, we'd have a huge detour. Jamie and Re were both in a good mood now but that wouldn't last for ever. They were tired and hungry. And so was I. I made my choice, shoved the map back in my rucksack and ran after them. I caught them up as they were looking at a statue of a woman with wild snake-like hair and a manic look on her face. Moss was growing out of her left nostril.

'Hey, Vicky – it's you!' Jamie quipped.

'Very funny.' I glanced at the statue again and couldn't help but smile. It had more than a passing resemblance to Charlene Slackton, I thought.

Chapter 15

At the end of the drive there was a big old house. When we saw it Vicky made us hide behind some bushes and creep along so if there was anyone inside and they were looking out of one of the windows, they wouldn't see us. It didn't look like a very friendly old house. On each side of the front door was a stone lion staring at us with its front paws stretched out. One of them only had one ear. I started counting the steps up to the door but Jamie said I'd better be quiet or the lions would come to life and eat me. Vicky said he was just making it up and told him to shut up. I stopped counting the steps.

Three big birds were sitting on a low roof at the end of the house. They weren't made of stone, they were greeny blue with long feathery tails. One of them swooped down near us making a squawky noise. I jumped behind Vicky.

'It's all right Re. They're only peacocks. They won't hurt you.'

I still didn't like them. Another one flew down and they both started pecking the ground near to where we were hiding. Their tails were so long they dragged on the ground behind them. Suddenly one of them lifted its tail up and spread it out like a big fan. The feathers had yellow and blue and green eyes. It was beautiful. Mrs Edwards helped us make fans at school when it was hot. It's quite difficult because you have to fold the paper one way then you turn it over and fold it the other way and then back the other way and so on until it looks like stairs when you open it out. I helped Maxine because she can't do folding. Some of her fingers don't work. They're twisted up. She can do colouring, just about, so we spent ages decorating them. Mine was purple because that's my favourite colour. It didn't have eyes on it but it did have some glitter that was left over from when we did snow pictures at Christmas. Mrs Edwards stapled the bottom edge for us so it made the fan shape. We took them into the playground at break-time but Charlene Slackton snatched them off us and squashed them into balls and threw them down the toilet and everyone laughed except me and Maxine and Mr Harris the caretaker because they got stuck down there and he had to put his special gloves on to get them out.

There was green stuff growing on the house. Vicky said it was ivy. It was everywhere. All over the walls and the roof. It was even growing over one of the lion's backs and up the front door and on some of the windows, covering them up. The rest of the windows were very small and dark with diamond shapes on the glass and the curtains were ripped. It looked the sort of house an evil old witch would live in.

'Maybe Mrs Frankish lives here.'

'Don't be daft Re. We're miles and miles away from home. It would take her hours to get to work every day.'

Not on her broomstick, I thought.

'I don't think anyone lives here any more,' said Vicky.

I wasn't sure about that. I looked up at one of the windows and saw the curtain move.

'Look, there she is!'

'Re – stop it!'

'But Mrs Frankish was peeping out from behind that curtain!'

I pointed up at the window. Some of the glass was missing and the curtain was blowing to and fro.

'It's just the wind Re,' said Vicky. 'There's no one there.'

'This place is really creepy,' said Jamie. 'Let's get out of here.'

Chapter 16

The gardens were totally wild and out of control, but underneath all the chaos and confusion it was a sad sort of place, forgotten and neglected. At one time, years ago, it must have been truly beautiful, somewhere people lavished time and effort and care. A real paradise. Now no one looked after it so it was slowly taking its revenge, putting up its own barriers: scratching, grazing and stinging anyone who dared to enter or try to explore it. I didn't blame it.

We tried to stay on what was left of a path that skirted the house and seemed to take us in the direction we needed to go but it was hard fighting through the scrub and bushes that blocked our way. Suffocating amongst the nettles and brambles that stung and scratched us were exotic-looking shrubs with sweet-smelling flowers and trees with strange patterned bark. Although we were alone in this jungle I kept having a weird feeling that someone else was there, following us, watching every move we made.

I didn't say anything to Jamie or Re and tried to push the thought out of my head. It wasn't easy. I told myself I was just being stupid. I was tired and my mind was playing tricks on me. I really didn't need to spook myself like this, I thought crossly. I already had plenty to worry about.

I felt better when we came out of the dense undergrowth into a large area of long knee-length grass. I guessed it must have once been a beautifully manicured lawn. In the centre was a large, rectangular, ornamental pond choked with water lilies and weeds.

Tramping down a path through the long grass like explorers, we made our way over to it and peered in.

'Wow!' Jamie shouted excitedly, leaning so far forward he looked as if he might fall headfirst into the pond any second.

Swimming under the canopy of water lily leaves were several ginormous fish. Each was at least a foot long, if not more. We sat down on the edge of the pond and watched them.

Jamie reached out his arm and trailed his hand in the water hoping the fish would come over to him.

'Watch they don't nibble your fingers off,' I joked.

It was Rhianna who heard them first. 'What's that?' she asked.

Jamie and I strained to listen. Then I heard it too. It was the sound of dogs, barking excitedly. It quickly became louder. A lot louder. They were coming in our direction.

We barely had time to scramble to our feet before they emerged from the bushes on the other side of the long grass: two huge and powerful alsatians bounding towards us. Re screamed.

'It's the lions!'

They stopped a few metres from us, staring threateningly with their ears pinned back, their teeth bared and their tails stretched out but not wagging.

'Go away!' shouted Jamie, waving his arms at them. 'Get lost!'

One of them started to growl, low and menacingly. I wasn't sure what to do but I knew we were in deep trouble. Dogs like these could be vicious. I'd read stories in the papers. They could injure. They could even kill.

'I don't like them!' Re wailed. 'I don't like them!'

Before I could stop her she'd turned to run.

'Stay where you are!' an authoritative voice called. A white-haired woman dressed in a light-blue raincoat tied at the waist with a piece of string emerged from behind one of the bushes. She was carrying a thin white stick.

'It's all right, Re. Do as she says. Stand still.'

Re looked at me, terrified, but did as she was told.

Then something odd happened. I'm not sure what the woman did – I didn't actually see her do anything, or say anything but the dogs suddenly stopped growling. One even started to wag its tail – not a friendly 'I'm pleased to see you' wag but a slow, suspicious, 'So who are you lot then?' wag.

'Now, very slowly walk over to me.'

We did as she said. The dogs made no attempt to follow us and once we were behind the woman it seemed as if they had lost interest in us. They bounded off, disappearing back in the bushes.

'Are you all right?' she asked.

Jamie and Re nodded but then, unable to stop myself, I burst into tears.

'You'd better come inside. I'll make some tea. Best thing for nasty shocks.' She took one of my nettle-stung hands in her own knobbly arthritic one and felt it with the other. 'And I suppose we'd better find something for those stings.'

Without another word, she turned and started walking back towards the house, stopping by a large clump of nettles.

'There's probably some dock leaves growing nearby,' she told us. 'If you pick them and rub them on your skin where you've been stung it'll help.'

I looked down and saw a clump of large green leaves. I picked a couple and handed them to her. 'Are these the ones?' I asked. She held them close to her face. 'That's them,' she said. We rubbed the leaves over our stings and it was lovely to get some relief from those painful white bumps.

'Those mutts don't belong to me, more's the pity. Be far better trained if they did. The people down in the lodge own them.' She waved her stick to indicate their direction. 'Too lazy to walk them. Let them roam free in my grounds. My brother would have words with them.' And with that she turned and went into the house.

Chapter 17

I wasn't sure I wanted to go past the lions into the old lady's house but Vicky said it would be all right. We went up the steps. Jamie patted one of the lions on its head and climbed up on its back.

'Nothing to be scared of Re. They're just stone. They won't bite. They won't do anything.'

'But you said —'

'I was only teasing.'

I went past them quickly and through the front door.

'Why's she got that stick?' I asked Vicky.

'I don't think she can see very well,' she whispered back. 'She uses it to feel her way around.'

I shut my eyes for a moment and took a few steps. I knocked into something hard and banged my side. It felt scary. I didn't know where I was. Vicky pulled my arm.

'What you doing Re?'

'Nothing.' I opened my eyes again and looked round.

The hall was full of old furniture. There were paintings on the walls of people in long time ago clothes, and piles of books and boxes of papers and the biggest piano I'd ever seen and a clock in a big case like in the Hickory Dickory Dock nursery rhyme. Everything was dusty. I don't think the old lady liked cleaning up much. I don't either. I'd much rather play with Baby Emma or my Barbies.

We went into the kitchen. There were saucepans hanging down from a rack over an old cooker and a white sink with a green stripy curtain round the bottom of it, a big table and chairs. The old lady picked up the kettle, felt for the tap then filled it and put it on top of the stove.

'I suppose you're hungry too,' she said.

'I'm starving!' I told her. 'We've only had doughnuts and apples today.'

'Doughnuts! Good grief . . . Is that what your parents feed you?' She shook her head then went over to the fridge. She opened the door and took out some shiny trays like take-away cartons.

I was just about to tell her that it wasn't our mum or dad that gave us the doughnuts when Vicky started talking very loudly and Jamie told me to shush.

'It's very kind of you,' said Vicky all politely. 'We don't usually have doughnuts . . . they were . . . a treat.'

'Well. That's something. You're growing. You need decent food.' The old lady looked down at the trays and sniffed. 'Meals on Wheels. Not exactly high cuisine but I don't know what I'd do without them.' She picked each tray up and putting it close to her eyes read the labels on the tops. 'I've got cottage pie, toad in the hole and . . . pasta.'

'Pasta please!' I said quickly. I didn't like the sound of the other things.

'But we can't eat your food,' Vicky said.

'Yes we can. She said we could!' I butted in quickly. I was starving.

The old lady laughed. 'It's quite all right my dear,' she said to Vicky as she put the trays into the oven. 'Marion'll be round tomorrow afternoon to drop off another lot. I'll just tell her I was hungry this week. She'll be very pleased. She's always saying I've got no appetite . . . Now my brother – he's a different kettle of fish. He could eat a horse and still have room for pud.'

'Eurgh. I wouldn't eat a horse,' I said. 'Even if I was really really hungry.'

The old lady laughed but I meant it.

Chapter 18

She'd been named Elizabeth Margaret after the Queen and her sister. When she was a child growing up during the Second World War, her family had lived on the outskirts of London in a big house, but because it had been so dangerous with all the bombs and air raids every night, she and her brother Lionel were evacuated. They hadn't wanted to leave their parents or each other but they'd had no choice. So, at the age of twelve, armed with a little box containing her gas mask and a small suitcase of clothes, she'd taken the train to Devon with the rest of the girls and teachers from her school. Her brother was sent to Canada on a ship called the *City of Benares*. It left Liverpool docks on 13th September 1940 with ninety children on board. By then Elizabeth was already in Devon. Lionel was just ten – the same age as Jamie.

As we sipped our tea, she took down an old brown tin

from a shelf with 'Sharpe's Toffees' written in gold lettering on the top and round the sides. It was full of curled, faded photos of her and her brother taken before the war.

'We were pretty much free range at your age. Especially in the school holidays. Out after breakfast, back when it got dark. Exploring usually. Every day with Lionel was an adventure.'

We looked through the photos together. They were happy smiling pictures, taken at the seaside or on picnics or at Christmas. Lionel was almost as tall as Elizabeth with blond hair, suntanned skin and a cheeky wide-mouthed grin.

'Well, this won't get the baby bathed,' said Elizabeth with a small sigh, getting up briskly. She went over to the oven. As she opened the door, heat filled the kitchen, which she wafted away with her frail bird-like arm.

'As ready as they'll ever be,' she said as she slowly took out the foil containers and put them on to the table. She told us where to get the plates and cutlery and I served up the food while Re and Jamie laid out the knives and forks.

We sat round the table and ate hungrily as Elizabeth poured herself another cup of tea and sipped it slowly.

I tried to say as little as possible about us but it was difficult. Elizabeth wasn't nosy or anything. It wasn't that. She didn't keep asking questions. In fact, she didn't really ask many at all but there was something about her. Something that made me let things slip. Things I wanted to keep hidden. I told her we hadn't meant to do anything wrong, we'd just got a bit lost and were taking a short cut through her grounds. She just nodded as if this sort of thing happened every day. Then it came out that we were heading for the station because we were going to our Great Aunt's house. Somehow, maybe because she'd told us all about being evacuated, and because Jamie was the same age as her brother when he was put on that ship to Canada, I started explaining about us being fostered and how we were going to be split up. She was quiet for a moment. I thought she was getting ready to tell us we'd better go straight back home. But she didn't.

'It's a terrible thing for a family to be separated. Not knowing whether you'll ever see people you love again,' she said softly.

We helped clear away the plates and I washed them up in the big stone sink. Jamie and Re wiped them dry and placed them back on the shelves.

Then Jamie asked if we could explore the house. I could tell he'd been itching to do this since we'd come inside.

Elizabeth smiled. 'It's not looking its best,' she said.

'We don't mind,' retorted Jamie and he was off in a flash.

It was a huge and rambling mansion just like the one from *The Lion, The Witch and The Wardrobe*, with long dark passages, heavy antique furniture and threadbare tapestries hanging from the walls. There was even a suit of armour, which freaked Re out but enthralled Jamie who was desperate to try it on. I put my foot down and told him no. There were nine bedrooms upstairs, two with four poster beds, complete with heavy moth-eaten curtains draped round them so they looked like huge holey tents. My friend Rosie would have had a field day. Every single room had its own fireplace, even the big old bathroom with its huge rusty-edged bath and cracked black and white tiles.

We were just about to go back downstairs when we saw a small door at the end of the passageway.

'Wonder what's through there,' said Jamie, quickly diving round the door. I followed him in and gasped. It was a boy's bedroom – the most amazing boy's room ever.

Laid out on the floor against the walls of the room ran a miniature train track complete with model bridges, tunnels, buildings, trees and people. Spaced around the track were about ten different engines each with an assortment of carriages and each one a detailed intricate replica of the real thing. On the chests of drawers there were models of ships, including a battleship, a pirate ship with sails and skull and crossbones flag and a passenger steamer with a big wheel attached to its side.

Hanging from the ceiling were models of old-fashioned aeroplanes, all covered in a film of dust but every one carefully made and painted. It was like Jamie had died and gone to heaven. He didn't know what to start with first.

We didn't hear Elizabeth come in.

'This is Lionel's room,' she said softly. 'He built all those planes himself.'

Jamie had already picked up one of the trains and was examining it.

'Will he mind if Jamie touches his stuff?' I asked quickly.

'Of course not,' she replied.

I looked round for Rhianna. She'd disappeared. Out in the hallway there was no sign or sound of her. I felt a slight twinge of panic.

'Re?' I called.

There was no answer.

'She won't have gone far,' said Elizabeth as we started checking all the upstairs rooms. 'Don't worry,' she added, realising I was getting anxious.

'You wouldn't think we were twins,' I told her. I explained that Re had been starved of oxygen when she was born. 'Nothing's easy for her. She can't manage on her own so I sort of have to help her with stuff.'

The old lady looked at me with her cloudy pale-blue eyes. 'Her time will come.'

I didn't understand. Re wasn't suddenly going to get a new brain and I didn't believe in miracle cures. So what did she mean?

We eventually found Re in one of the spare bedrooms in the four-poster bed, curled up and fast asleep under a beautiful golden silky eiderdown. On the pillow next to her lay a small china ornament about three inches tall. A black and white penguin with a cheeky smile and a pink bow tie.

I leaned forward to take it but Elizabeth stopped me.

'It's all right. Don't wake Sleeping Beauty,' she whispered with a smile.

It did seem cruel to wake her. I glanced out of the window. It was beginning to get dark. We should have left hours ago. The peacocks were screeching as they prepared to settle down for the night. I wondered if the people in the lodge had let their dogs loose again. I thought I could hear them barking in the distance. The garden no longer looked like a jungle; it was just a tangled mass of black shadows. Anything could be lurking out there. I wasn't looking forward to leaving – I was dreading it.

I didn't want to be the one in charge any more, sorting everything and everyone out. I just wanted to be an ordinary fourteen-year-old kid with no decisions bigger than whether to buy a teen mag or a bar of chocolate.

I sighed. I felt completely lost.

'You can stay here tonight if you think that's best,' said Elizabeth.

I nodded. Relieved.

'Thank you.'

Elizabeth hesitated then took my hand in hers.

'Come with me. I want to show you something,' she said.

We went downstairs into the sitting room. There was a dusty old bureau in the corner of the room. Propping her white stick against it, she flopped down the lid and fumbled inside, finally pulling out an old paper folder. Inside was a single, yellow, slightly mildewed newspaper cutting. She handed it to me. It was dated 28th September 1940. There was a black and white photo of the ship the *City of Benares*.

I looked at Elizabeth. She gave a small firm nod. I read on. The ship had been torpedoed by a German submarine six hundred miles out at sea. Only seven of the ninety evacuee children had survived.

'My brother wasn't one of those lucky seven, unfortunately. He never got to Canada and he never came home.' Her voice was full of sadness and regret. 'There's not a single day goes by that I don't think about him.' She looked me in the eye. 'Vicky, I'm an old woman. Lots has changed since I was your age. But some things stay the same and are always important – brothers and sisters, parents . . . families. You have a choice about what you do. You can choose to go on . . . or you can go back. It's up to you and I can't tell you what's best. But there's one thing I will say: desperate times call for desperate measures.'

Chapter 19

It was funny waking up in Elizabeth's house. It was cosy and warm in the bed. I didn't want to get up. I wanted to stay under the lovely silky yellow cover but Vicky was already up and putting on her trainers.

'Come on, Re, time to get out of bed,' she said.

'I don't want to. I'm tired.' I picked up the little penguin on my pillow and stroked its shiny head.

'We've got a train to catch. The sooner we get going, the sooner we get to Great Auntie Irene's.'

'But I'm really really tired.'

'You can have a big sleep when we get to Great Auntie Irene's. You can sleep for a whole week if you like!'

'I want to sleep now.'

Vicky sat down on the edge of the bed and looked at me. 'Don't you remember how much you loved it when we were there on holiday?'

I nodded.

'Well it's going to be like that but even better. Because we're going to live there, it'll be like we're on holiday all the time.'

'Really?'

Vicky nodded. 'Every single day,' she said.

I got up out of the bed and pulled on my trainers. A holiday every single day. I liked that idea.

Jamie was already downstairs with Elizabeth. He was eating cornflakes.

'All set?' Elizabeth asked, looking at Vicky.

Vicky nodded and grinned.

'Thank you,' she said. 'For everything.' She gave Elizabeth a hug.

'You've got a good head on those shoulders. I know you'll use it. Your Great Aunt is a very lucky woman.'

We picked up our rucksacks. I still had the little penguin in my hand. I held it out to Elizabeth.

'This is yours,' I said.

She felt it with her wrinkly hand.

'Keep it,' she said with a smile. 'He might bring you luck.'

'Thank you,' I said. I popped him into my coat pocket and zipped it up so he couldn't fall out and I wouldn't lose him.

We all walked down through the garden along a windy path, past a little stream. It was a very big garden. It was bigger than the park at home and much much nicer. There were no smashed up fridges in the bushes or beer cans on the grass.

We went down another little road with more statues till we got to some big gates. Next to one of the gates was a little house. Elizabeth said this was the lodge. Inside we could hear dogs barking.

'It's all right,' Elizabeth told us, 'the owners lock them up during the day while they're out.'

She told us how to get to the station and we all said goodbye and she hugged us and then leaned on her stick and watched us walk off down the road. I looked back after a while. She was still there. She was very small like a little bird. She gave us one last wave and then we went round the bend and we couldn't see her any more.

It took a long time to get to the station. Vicky showed me where we were going on the map – it didn't look far but it took ages. I was getting fed up and wanted to sit down and have a rest but bossy old Vicky said I couldn't. She said we had to keep going.

I'd never been on a train before. At the station the man behind the glass gave us our tickets and said, 'Enjoy your trip.' Vicky and Jamie went over to the board to check what time our train was. I sat down on a bench to wait for them and took my penguin out of my pocket but then this man came up and sat down next to me.

'Hello,' he said. 'That's a nice little penguin.'

'I know,' I said.

'Do you like animals?' he asked.

I nodded.

'So do I,' he said. 'But I like real ones best. I've got some lovely puppies back at my house. They're only a few weeks old. I don't suppose you like puppies though . . .'

'Oh yes . . . I love them,' I said.

Then Vicky came over. I don't know why but the man got up and hurried out of the station and down the street. Vicky took my hand and pulled me towards the toilets.

'But I've just been Vicky!' I told her but she still rushed me in there.

'I'm not a baby. I don't need to go every two seconds,' I told her.

She didn't take any notice. She just started filling up our drinks bottles from the tap. 'You mustn't talk to anyone, Re, not a word!'

'You can't tell me what to do – you're not Mum. Anyway I was only doing a conversation. Mrs Edward says doing a conversation is a Life Skill.'

'I don't care what Mrs Edwards says!'

'I'll tell her you said that.'

Vicky made a groaning noise. 'Stuff Mrs Edwards,' she said. 'Come on. The train'll be here any minute.'

I was really cross with her. She was always bossing me around. I went back into one of the toilets and sat down on the seat.

'Re!' she yelled. 'Come on.'

I didn't budge.

'What's the matter now?'

'I'm not talking to you,' I said. 'And I'm not doing anything you say. So put that in your nuckets and smoke it.'

Chapter 20

'Rhianna!'

'I can't hear you . . .' She put her hands over her ears and started singing to herself. Something told me this wasn't going to be easy.

'Please, Rhianna, not now . . .' She turned her back on me. Outside on the platform I could hear the tannoy announcing our train. What if Jamie got on and we were left here? I glanced through the open window and saw him right at the end of the crowded platform. He was too far away for me to call out without having to shout – we couldn't afford to draw attention to ourselves.

'Rhianna, you've got to come, right now. I mean it!' I could hear my voice getting tighter and tighter, and her tuneless singing getting louder and louder. This wasn't going to work. I looked through the window at Jamie again then back to Re. She was so infuriating sometimes; I could throttle her. I knew I couldn't force her out on to the platform – she was much bigger and stronger than me – and if I tried, she'd throw a wobbly. There was only one thing to do. It was going to be a gamble but I had no choice. I took a deep breath and fought hard to keep my voice sounding light and unconcerned.

'OK, Re. You stay here. That's fine. I'm going on the train with Jamie.' I turned to go. 'Bye, then . . .'

The singing faltered slightly but I knew I had to call her bluff. I kept on going, desperately resisting the temptation to turn round. I forced my legs to walk through the door. Outside on the platform there were crowds of people waiting. The stationmaster was helping an old couple with their suitcases. I avoided his eye and sidled past him towards Jamie. The train pulled up and he eagerly bounded forward. I called to him to hang on but it was too late; he hadn't heard and was already scrambling aboard.

I rushed up to the train, my palms sweating and my heart pounding. I looked round. No sign of Re. Jamie appeared at the window inside one of the carriages and grinned.

'Where's Rhianna?' he mouthed through the glass.

I felt sick. The panic was rising. How could I have been so stupid to leave her on her own in that toilet? What was I thinking of and what on earth was I going to do now? I tried to motion to Jamie to get off the train but he thought I was telling him to put his bag on the luggage rack and turned away. People streamed around me but I was rooted to the spot. I just didn't know what to do. Who should I go after – Re or Jamie? In a few more seconds the train doors would close, and the train would pull away, taking Jamie with it, but if I leapt on, it would mean leaving Re on her own and that didn't bear thinking about. But would Jamie know what to do if the train went off without us? He wasn't the most clued-up kid in the world.

I had to stay with Re and get Jamie off the train. I started to bang on the window. A man in a beige suit turned and glared disapprovingly at me. I smiled apologetically and he tutted and shook his head, muttering to a woman in a green coat. At this rate, we'd be discovered any second but I had to do something. Ignoring the man, I started thumping frantically on the window again. Suddenly I felt a hand on my shoulder and froze.

I turned round, expecting to be confronted by the angry stationmaster, but to my relief I saw Re standing in front of me, her face blotchy and red.

'Don't ever do that again!' I hissed, yanking her hand off my shoulder. She reeled back as if I'd hit her. Tears started to roll down her bewildered moon face.

'I'm sorry, Vicky. I'm sorry.'

She was shaking and so was I. I put my arm tightly round her and bit my lip till I could taste blood. 'It's OK. Don't cry any more.'

The guard blew his whistle as the last few passengers got on. I hurried Re on to the train and looked round for Jamie. He was standing at the end of the now crowded carriage.

'What took you so long?' he asked, staring at me accusingly.

Most of the seats were taken so we made our way into the next carriage. Re had finally stopped crying but was hiccupping noisily. She wouldn't let go of my hand, and in a way I didn't want her to.

The train was packed with half-term holidaymakers and nobody really noticed us. Eventually we found a table between four seats. A man with a beard was sitting in the far corner. In front of him, he had a little radio, which was reporting the cricket. I hate cricket, it's sooooo boring. He must have thought so too. His eyes were tight shut and he was snoring really loudly. We sank down in the three spare seats and, for the first time that day, I allowed myself to relax.

I looked out of the window while Re chatted happily to Jamie, her tears forgotten. We drank the water out of our bottles – it tasted disgusting but we were all so thirsty we didn't care any more. We were on our way, whizzing out of the town, past endless fields and woods, then a river with men fishing, horses grazing and a family out picnicking.

Gradually the countryside became wilder and craggier and bare hills loomed in the distance. The rhythm of the train seemed to be saying, 'You're nearly there, you're nearly there.' We stopped at some stations – people got off but loads more got on to replace them. Each time the train started up its reassuring chant again. 'You're nearly there, you're nearly there, you're nearly there.'

Guiltily, I thought of Paul and Sarah. It was horrible

not knowing what was happening. Please, please, please let their baby be OK, I thought. I imagined them in the hospital, Paul sitting by Sarah's bed waiting for her to wake up, or waiting for the doctors to come round, or encouraging her to eat something. I knew the routine. I'd done it with Mum. I hoped they were too caught up in their own troubles to worry too much about us. An uncomfortable thought struck me. Dad would know by now too. What would he be thinking?

I forced myself to think of something else. Matt. No. Rosie? I desperately wanted to text or ring her but I'd deliberately kept my phone switched off. I knew the police could trace calls. It was much too risky.

I shut my eyes and decided that I had to think positive. To look forwards, not backwards. When we got to Great Auntie Irene's, she'd be surprised to see us of course but she'd give us something good to eat and tell us everything was going to be all right from now on and I didn't need to worry any more. She might have been really old but she had all her marbles and she'd sort everything out. When we were first taken away from Dad, Mrs Frankish had asked if we had any other family who could look after us. There was only Uncle Mac or Great Auntie Irene. Uncle Mac runs a sheep farm somewhere in Australia and Mrs Frankish said we weren't going there. When she found out Great Auntie Irene was eighty-one and didn't have a phone, she said staying with her wasn't an option and we weren't to bother her.

I should never have listened to the old bat – Great Auntie Irene was family.

It really would be like a fantastic holiday, I thought. Better even. It would be like coming home. A proper home. And, if we could never go back to Paul and Sarah's, it wouldn't be the end of the world. We'd make a new life, start new schools and make new friends – no one like Rosie maybe, but she was a one-off. Re would come on leaps and bounds with Great Auntie Irene's help. She loved reading stories with her. And Jamie would settle down at last. He'd finally stop whacking people. He was always so gentle with Jip – that dog brought out the soft side of him. They'd play together for hours in Auntie's huge garden and he'd make loads of dens and camps but she wouldn't mind a bit. She was like that. Maybe she'd even let us camp out on the island again. And we'd help her too – earn our keep with the chores like shopping or cleaning. Even Re could help wash up or lay the table so us being there would be good for her too. And we'd be company.

'Old people get lonely,' Great Auntie Irene told me once. 'We like to have you youngsters around to shake things up a bit and remind us we're still alive!'

I thought of Elizabeth back in her huge mansion with just her memories for company. We could go back and see her. Visit. Take Great Auntie Irene. The pair would get on like a house on fire. They'd be swapping wartime memories like there was no tomorrow. I smiled to myself. Everything was going to be perfect.

I opened my eyes. Re and Jamie were playing noughts and crosses on a scrap of paper. Jamie was letting her win for a change and she had a big grin on her face. The radio was still on but the cricket seemed to have given way to the news. I double-checked our map, mentally ticking off the stations we'd already stopped at and planning our route when we got off at the station after the next one. Suddenly something the newsreader said made me sit up sharp.

'. . . the three missing children, non-identical twin girls aged fourteen and a boy of ten . . .'

I froze. Jamie and Re hadn't heard. The newsreader began to describe our exact appearance. Hardly daring, I glanced over to the people sitting on the other side of the aisle. They were chatting and laughing at the moment but how long would it take one of them to notice us? I quickly reached over and flicked the radio off. The man with the beard immediately started to stir.

'Quick, get up,' I urged Jamie and Rhianna.

'What's the matter?' asked Jamie.

The man picked up his radio, puzzled at its abrupt silence. He shook it, then realising it had been turned off, glared at us, switched it on again even louder, giving us another rude stare.

'Appeals for the children to return home have so far been unsuccessful and police are becoming increasingly concerned for their welfare and safety. And now the weather . . .'

Jamie went white and grabbed his bag. I got Re to her feet and started ushering her out of the carriage following Jamie. We passed a woman in a red jumper who glanced up at the three of us.

There was a flicker of surprise in her expression. She looked as if she was about to say something but I didn't wait around to listen; I bundled Jamie and Re into the next carriage. The train was coming into a station.

'What's the matter, Vicky?' Re asked.

'We've got to get off now, Re. Right now.'

'But we've only done five stations. I counted. You said six.'

'Never mind. Come on. Bring your bag.'

We moved quickly through the carriages to the other end of the train and when it came to a halt and we could finally open the door, we leapt out.

It was a tiny station surrounded by countryside in the middle of nowhere, with large pots full of bright red geraniums and a white picket fence. It was very quiet and completely deserted except for a few hikers in shorts and walking boots, who got off at the same time as us.

I looked back at the train – the woman in the red jumper was on the platform talking urgently to the guard and pointing at us. She had recognised us all right. The guard was torn between moving the train off and chasing after us. As we ran to the exit tumbling through the group of hikers, she called after us, 'Come back!' but we didn't.

We were nearly at Great Auntie Irene's. We were nearly there. We couldn't give up now.

Chapter 21

When we ran out of the station, Vicky made us hide in some bushes so she could have a look at the map again. She said because we got off the train early it was going to take us a bit longer to get to Great Auntie Irene's but it would be all right because we were going to take a short cut. I didn't think it was very short. We went down a footpath. There were no houses just fields and hedges and trees and lots of sheep with muddy bottoms that baa-ed and clattered away noisily if we went near them.

We walked for ages and ages and the brambles scratched my legs and my feet were sore and I kept tripping up and banging my knees when we climbed over gates. Then it started raining and my hood wouldn't stay up so my hair got wet and water trickled all down my neck and I wanted to go back to Elizabeth's house. I told Vicky but she wasn't listening because she was looking at the map and arguing with Jamie about which way to go. Then Jamie said we had to watch out for adders. One little bite and our mouths would start foaming and our arms and legs would jerk and we would die if we didn't get the right medicine.

Once in the Unit, one of Maxine's arms and legs started jerking and she had foamy spit coming out of her mouth. I don't think it was an adder bite though. We've only got guinea pigs in the Unit. They're called Floppy and Tom and I don't think they're poisonous. Mrs Edwards didn't say what it was. She didn't say anything except we all had to go out into the corridor and wait. I didn't want to because I saw Maxine looking at me and I knew she wanted me to stay with her and hold the hand which wasn't jerking but they wouldn't let me. An ambulance came. Even Charlene Slackton stopped laughing and stared with her mouth open when they put Maxine in the back. It was break-time and everyone was watching. They put the siren on and all the Year Seven boys chased the van out of the gates. Maxine didn't come back to school for ages.

I was fed up with running away. So was Jamie. He was getting crosser and crosser. He snatched the map out of Vicky's hands and said she was just a stupid girl and everyone knew girls couldn't read maps. He looked at it for ages and ages and when Vicky said, OK, where are we then, he threw it back at her and said how should he know.

Vicky was really angry because she didn't catch the map when he threw it at her. It fell on the ground and got all wet and muddy and then it started to blow away and she had to chase it and, when she caught it, it was ripped.

She told Jamie off but he just shouted really really rude words at her and told her he didn't care.

My jeans were all covered in mud and I was cold and my socks were soggy. I told Vicky but she said it was all right because we'd be there soon. But we weren't. We just kept on walking. And walking. And walking.

When we did the sponsored walk in the Unit to raise money for our own computer we never walked this far. It was sunny and we had drinks and snacks and Mrs Edwards played I Spy with us as we went along and we sang songs and it was fun. I didn't want to sing songs or play I Spy even though Vicky said I could do all the spying.

I kept asking Vicky if we were there yet and she kept saying 'In a little while' or 'Nearly' but we still weren't and after a while she stopped saying anything at all when I asked her. Jamie told me to shut up moaning or he'd give me a double chinese burn and whack me. Vicky still didn't say anything so I sat down on the wet grass. Then she said something.

'Re what the hell are you doing?'

'I want my dinner.'

'We haven't got any dinner. Come on, get up!' She bent down over me and tried to pull me up.

I pushed her off. 'I want sausages, chips and peas and then I want to watch Neighbours with Great Auntie Irene.'

'Get up!' Vicky shouted.

'What's the point?' Jamie said, chucking his rucksack on to the ground next to me. 'This is stupid. We don't know

where we are – we could be going anywhere! We're probably going round and round in circles thanks to you!'

'Me? Hang on, you're the ones that wanted to run
away!' Vicky snapped. 'I never wanted to go anywhere,
remember? This is all your big idea.' She stared down at us
both sitting on the grass in the rain. Her orange hair was
like wet wool and bits were stuck to her face. 'Get up!
We've got to keep going!'

'Stop bossing us around!' yelled Jamie back at her.
'We're fed up with it, aren't we Re?'

'Yeah. You're always bossing us. We don't like it.'

She looked at us both then made a funny sort of gulping
noise.

'Bossing you around?' she said. Her face was all red and
her mouth was twisted up. 'OK. That's fine. I'll stop bossing
you around. Stay right here if you like. It's not my job to
watch over you. I'm not Mum. Understand? I'm not her.'
She wiped the wet hair from her face. 'And something else.
I'm tired and I'm hungry and I'm soaked to the skin too. I've
had enough. So from now on you can do what you like. So
I won't be bossing either of you around any more because,
guess what? I'm going back. And I don't care what happens
to us all. They can split us up. They can send me to the
moon. I just don't care any more . . .'

As she turned round and started to walk away Jamie got
up and ran at her, growling like a bear. He jumped on her
back and she tried to push him off. She swung round and
started yelling at him to leave her alone but he wouldn't.
They fell on the ground rolling round and round in the wet

mud, whacking and shouting and screaming at each other.

The noise stabbed into my ears and screeched round inside my head till it hurt. I shouted at them to stop but they wouldn't so I started yelling too. I ran off up the hill. I shut my eyes and put my hands over my ears to try to keep out the noise. I kept running up and up until my legs wobbled underneath me and I started falling, slipping and tumbling down I didn't know where.

Chapter 22

We both heard the scream. Startled, we looked up, our fight forgotten.

'Rhianna!'

There was no sign of her. We ran full pelt up the hill. Reaching the peak we hardly dared to look down the other side. The ground fell away sharply and the steep slope was studded with trees, scrub and brambles. And then we saw her at the bottom, close to a boulder-filled stream. She was lying on the ground like a limp rag doll. We rushed down the slope, half sliding, half running, tearing our clothes and grazing our skin. I could feel the panic rising. We were miles from anywhere. What if she was seriously hurt? Suddenly I felt sick. What if she were dead?

I stopped and stared at her. She was so still. Her big moon face was splattered with dirt but white as chalk. Was this how dead people looked? I never saw Mum after she died. One evening she was in her bed at the hospital, the next morning she was gone and Dad was clearing her things out of the little locker. He'd said Jamie was too young and Re wouldn't understand but I should go to the funeral with him. But I just couldn't bear to see the coffin with Mum shut up inside it so I never went. I never said goodbye.

Jamie got to Re first. He bent down close to her face.

'She's breathing,' he whispered. 'Vicky, don't just stand there . . .'

But I didn't know what to do. This was my worst nightmare and it was all my fault.

'Vicky!' Jamie shouted. 'Do something!'

I pulled off my jacket, made it into a cushion and gently tucked it under her head. I got some tissues from my rucksack, wet them in the stream and gently wiped the mud and dirt from her face. After a few seconds her eyelids fluttered a little.

'Re, are you OK?'

She opened her eyes and groaned.

'Where are you hurt?' asked Jamie.

'Everywhere.'

'It's all right, you're going to be all right.' I looked at Jamie. His face was as pale as Rhianna's. He looked like he was going to cry any minute.

Slowly, bit by bit, we got her to gently move each finger and toe, each arm and leg. Nothing was broken and the worst of it seemed to be cuts and bruises, but she was exhausted.

'We've got to get her out of this rain,' I said.

I looked round. The opposite slope was steeper and faced with bare rock. A small waterfall cascaded down it into a fern-edged rock pool. The stream flowed down from this pool winding its way between moss-covered rocks and round trees. A little way past the waterfall, the rock face jutted out, creating a small dark hollow at ground level. Thinking this might give us some shelter from the rain, I pointed it out to Jamie and he went over to investigate. He disappeared out of sight for a few seconds then reappeared with the trace of a nervous grin on his face.

'It's a cave! It's half covered up with brambles and it's not very big but it's dry inside. Someone's used it as a den before – there's stuff still in it.'

We helped Rhianna up and, putting our arms round her for support, managed to get her to the cave. We carefully pulled back a ton of brambles and the branches of a huge wild rose bush with pink flowers. The outside walls were dripping with ferns and moss, but inside, just like Jamie promised, it was dry. I shivered knowing that it must have been stuffed full of spiders and other lovely creepy crawlies but for Re's sake I didn't allow myself to think about them.

Inside, there was a dusty matted rug on the floor and even a couple of mouldy cushions. We sat Rhianna gently down on the floor, took off her wet coat and jeans and wrapped her sleeping bag round her. On a little rocky shelf there was an old biscuit tin and a few tatty comics. Everything looked as if it hadn't been touched for ages. Gingerly, I opened the tin. Inside there was half a packet of stale biscuits. We were so hungry we ate every last crumb.

I used some of the water from the stream to clean up Re's cuts as best I could. Then we unrolled our sleeping bags and gently zipped Re into hers.

'Re,' I whispered as I snuggled her down, 'I'm sorry. Those things I said. I didn't mean them. I do care about you both. Honest.'

She looked at me with those wide-set grey eyes, then asked, 'Are you going to leave us here on our own?'

'Course not, silly,' I replied, giving her a big hug.

'I'm not silly.'

'You're right,' I told her. 'I'm the silly one.'

After hanging up our wet coats and jeans to dry as best we could, Jamie and I lay down either side of Rhianna and within a few minutes she was fast asleep. Ten minutes later Jamie was asleep too. It had been such a long, horrible day. I turned over and shut my eyes but sleep wouldn't come. It wasn't quite dark yet but the rain had stopped and the clouds were clearing away. As quietly as I could, I unzipped my sleeping bag, pulled on my spare jeans and wet trainers and clambered out of the cave.

It was very quiet and the ground smelt fresh and earthy. I followed the path of the stream down through the woods, thinking that I could easily retrace my steps as long as it wasn't too dark. The woods were strangely silent and eerie. The air was misty and the leaves on the trees were shiny and dripping. I followed the stream for about ten minutes and was just about to turn back when the trees thinned and the ground became more pebbly. I looked up and gasped when I saw it. Our island on the lake. Right in front of me.

We'd been so close but hadn't even realised it was there. The lake was as beautiful as I remembered – the surface of the water shimmered pinks and oranges in the sunset.

I hurried down to the shore and looked up along the lake edge. Perched halfway up a hill was the house where Great Auntie Irene lived with Jip. It sat with its green paintwork and grey tiled roof like an old friend patiently waiting for us. This was going to be our perfect new home.

I wanted to shout and whoop and cry all at the same time but I didn't dare. In the distance, I could hear the high-pitched whine of a couple of dirt bikes. There were still people around.

It was late now. I didn't want to give Great Auntie Irene a fright this time of night. She was an old lady and probably didn't get many visitors.

I heard Jip bark excitedly a few times as some quacking ducks splash-landed on the lake. I didn't feel like going back to the cave, I wanted to sit looking at the house and the lake and the island all night but it was almost dark and I knew I must. The last thing I needed now was to get lost or lose my footing and fall over, so slowly and carefully I retraced my steps back along the stream to the cave. Jamie and Re were still sound asleep.

'We're here,' I whispered quietly into the darkness. 'We really are here.'

Chapter 23

In the morning, Jamie said to hurry and get up because we were going to see Great Auntie Irene but when I got out of my sleeping bag my legs felt all wobbly and tired. My jeans were nearly dry but I didn't feel like hurrying anywhere, even to see Great Auntie Irene and Jip, but Vicky said I'd probably feel better in a little while and gave me a drink of water from her bottle. She checked my cuts and bruises and kept asking me if I felt dizzy.

We followed the stream. I nearly fell in because it was slippery and Vicky and Jamie had to help me. After a while we came out of the woods and could see the lake. Jamie and I started to cheer and shout hurray until Vicky said we had to be quiet, just in case. I wanted to go down to the water but Vicky said, 'No, look.' She was pointing to Great Auntie Irene's house. I felt so happy I forgot I was tired. We ran along the lake edge until we saw a path.

'Come on,' Jamie said. 'It leads straight to the house, remember?'

We were nearly at the bottom of Great Auntie's garden when we saw the back door open and a lady come out. She had curly black hair and dark brown skin.

'She looks like Maxine's mum!' I whispered to Vicky.

'Must be a visitor,' she said. 'Or maybe it's someone who helps out with chores or something.'

'She won't need her any more with us around,' I said.

A tall man with yellow hair followed her out of the house carrying a large cardboard box.

'Who's that then?' I asked.

'They're burgling her,' said Jamie. 'Come on!'

He climbed over the gate and into Great Auntie's back garden as the lady and man walked round the side of the house. Jamie started running.

'Jamie wait . . .'

Vicky and I followed him, but by the time we got to the house the burglars had got into a red car and were driving off.

'They've probably tied her up. We've got to help her,' yelled Jamie.

We went up to the back door. Vicky slowly pushed it open. It creaked like doors always do in scary films.

'Great Auntie Irene . . .?' she called quietly.

There was no one in the kitchen. The house was quiet. The kitchen looked different. Great Auntie Irene used to have a big cupboard with shelves on top with lots of pretty cups and plates and a big brown teapot and two china cats with a photo of us lot between them. It had all vanished like magic. Instead of Jip's old basket there was a big furry cushion on the floor.

'Where is she Vicky?' I said. 'I want Great Auntie Irene.'

The door to the hallway started to open – Great Auntie Irene had heard us at last.

But it wasn't her. It was a boy. A tall boy with toffee-coloured skin and jumpy brown eyes.

'What have you done with Great Auntie Irene?' said Jamie, going up close and sticking his face into the boy's. The boy stepped backwards.

'Nothing . . . Who are you?'

'We're her relatives and we've come to see her.'

'I don't know what you're on about.' His voice went all shaky. 'This is my house – you'd better get out before my parents get back or —'

'But she lives here.'

'No she doesn't!'

Then Jip came bounding through the kitchen door.

'Jip!'

Jamie knelt down and gave him a big cuddle. Jip licked him excitedly.

'His name's Max.'

Jamie moved over to the other side of the kitchen and said 'Jip!' The dog ran to him.

'See. His name's Jip. He belongs to our auntie.'

'Max,' called the boy. The dog turned and bounded back. 'I found him just after we moved in. He was hanging around outside the back door, pawing and whining to come in. He was half starved and his coat was all matted.' He looked at Vicky. 'Mum thinks he must have belonged to the old lady who lived here before us.'

'So where is she now?'

The boy pushed his shoulders up and down.

'I think she died . . .'

Chapter 24

I sank down on a nearby chair.

'Where's Great Auntie Irene?' Re asked.

'She's not here, Re. She's dead,' I said quietly. Rhianna started to cry.

Jamie kicked the table and thumped it hard with his fist. 'It's not fair!'

'D'you mind —' the boy started, but Jamie swung round and glared at him fiercely from under his dark caterpillar eyebrows. Warily, the boy took another step back. He looked about my age or a bit older but Jamie was pretty scary when he was angry.

'So what are we going to do now?' Jamie asked, glaring at me.

I sighed. I didn't feel like stating the blooming obvious. It was all over. Finished. We'd have to go back. Re would go to the residential school and Jamie and I would be farmed out with strangers. We probably wouldn't see each other for months.

The boy was glancing nervously at Jamie as if he might bite him at any moment.

'So . . . What's going on?'

I looked at the boy. Perhaps there was a way. Maybe this wasn't the end of our adventure.

'Can you keep a secret?' I blurted out.

The boy shrugged, puzzled. 'Course.'

'Don't tell him anything,' snapped Jamie.

'My name's Daniel.'

I looked at him and suddenly the doubts rose up in me. Could I trust him? His eyes darted warily between us, as if he was expecting trouble. Then I remembered what Elizabeth had said about desperate times calling for desperate measures. I made my choice.

'We've run away.'

Daniel turned and stared at me. I could feel myself going bright red. His face suddenly changed, his eyes opening wide. 'You're those Davies kids, aren't you? I saw your pictures on the telly last night. Everyone's looking for you.'

'We're not going back.'

'My mum and dad'll be home any minute.'

'They mustn't see us. They mustn't know anything about us.'

'But —'

'We've found a cave —' started Rhianna.

'That's my cave!'

'It's ours now,' Jamie interrupted, glaring at Daniel fiercely.

Outside there were sounds of a car drawing up.

'Will you help us?' I begged him. 'Please . . .'

He looked uncomfortably from Jamie to me to Rhianna.

The doors of a car slammed. Rhianna started to wail loudly and embarrassingly.

'Not now, Re, for goodness' sake!'

'But I don't want to go to that school. I want to stay with you and Jamie.'

The boy pulled a face. Something had helped him make his decision.

'OK . . . I'll help. But you'll have to be quick – and quiet.'

Rhianna stopped her noise and he led us through the hall and into the living room. Quickly, he unlocked and opened the French windows.

'Daniel?' a woman's voice called from the kitchen.

'Coming!' He turned to us. 'Stay at the cave. They don't know about it. No one does. I'll bring you some food and stuff as soon as I can.'

Before I could stop her, Rhianna dived forward and threw her arms round him in a big bear hug. 'Thank you!'

The boy grinned, and for a moment his sad eyes lit up and he looked like a different person.

Quickly he unhooked himself from Rhianna. 'Just don't mess up my cave, all right?'

As Re nodded, Daniel's mum called him again from the hall.

'Now go!' he urged, hurrying us into the garden.

Chapter 25

Daniel brought us tons of food – pork pies, bananas, jaffa cakes (my favourite), cheese, bread rolls, potatoes, milk, orange juice and loads of other stuff. Yum. He even brought plates, cups and some knives and forks and spoons.

We were so hungry but do you know, bossy old Vicky made us wait till we'd swept out the cave for spiders and put our sleeping bags out over the bushes to get any bugs out.

We made the cave really cosy – Daniel and Jamie pulled the floor rug outside and we each held a corner and waved it up and down and banged it with our hands and a big cloud of dust came out of it making us sneeze and cough. When we couldn't get any more dust out of it we took it back inside the cave and spread it out on the floor again. We put all the food and the plates and stuff up on the shelf. There was room for my little penguin, my Furby, my baldy

Barbies, Baby Emma with the poked out eyes and my disco lamp too. I was glad I brought my lamp even though there wasn't anywhere to plug it in. Vicky's torch didn't work any more but Jamie said I could borrow his torch and shine it behind the lamp. I picked some of the pink flowers and put them on the shelf too in a cup with some water. I put the photo of us all next to the flowers then I gave Baby Emma a bath in the stream and put her outside the cave on a bush to dry in the sunshine.

We had pork pie and bananas for breakfast. Vicky said it wasn't really breakfast because it must have been nearly lunch-time and when we'd finished we were still hungry so we ate all the jaffa cakes too.

'Beats school dinner,' Jamie said doing one of his mega burps. Vicky told him off for being disgusting but then Daniel did an even bigger burp. Jamie looked impressed. No one can do burps louder than him. Not even Ollie Stanmore.

But Vicky didn't tell Daniel off. She didn't say anything at all.

'You haven't told Daniel off,' I said but she wasn't listening. She was just smiling at Daniel like I wasn't there or something.

'Vicky you haven't told Daniel off. Tell him off too or it's not fair on Jamie.'

She made a face at me. Her eyes went all big and staring.

'Why are you making that face?' She still didn't answer and she made her teeth all gritty. 'Jamie why's Vicky making that funny face?'

Jamie shrugged. 'P'raps she's trying to do a burp and it's got stuck halfway.'

He started laughing. Daniel looked at Vicky. She stopped making the funny face and looked down.

'In some countries it's really rude if you don't burp,' he said quickly. 'Means you think the meal was rubbish.'

I tried to do a big burp too but it came out wrong. Everyone just laughed and Jamie said I sounded like a frog with a sore throat.

'What's your school like?' I asked Daniel. He didn't say anything for a bit then he just poked the ground with a stick.

'I don't go to school any more,' he said really quietly.

'Everyone goes to school,' I said.

'I don't.'

'So what makes you so different?' asked Jamie in his watch out or I'll whack you voice.

'My mum and dad teach me at home. They're allowed.'

'I bet,' said Jamie.

Jip went up to Daniel and nuzzled his leg. He got up. 'I'm taking Max down to the lake,' he said without looking at us.

Chapter 26

There wasn't anyone at the lake. That was what I'd loved when we'd stayed at Great Auntie Irene's – we hardly ever used to see a soul, just the occasional boat pottering by or a bedraggled hiker, lost because he'd strayed off the usual walkers' paths. Most people stuck to the other shore where the road ran all the way along the lakeside up to the town.

It was calm and sunny today, with no wind to ripple the dark velvety water, and the island stood lush and green about thirty metres away.

Poor Great Auntie Irene. I couldn't believe that we would never see her again. Upside down, near the water's edge lay her old dinghy. It was pretty ropey years ago but now it looked even more battered and forlorn than ever, with its paint flaking off like old scabs and its name – *Guinevere* – half rubbed away.

'Vicky look!' called Rhianna, plonking herself down on its upturned hull. 'Mum used to sit here by this boat and watch us play, remember?'

'Yeah. Mind you don't fall off.'

'I won't. Don't fuss.'

I bit my lip. Fussing was easier than remembering. Jamie looked on enviously as Daniel threw Jip a stick. He bounced eagerly into the lake, creating splashes of white spray and then swimming back with the stick in his mouth, just his head visible. He laid it at Daniel's feet, shook himself madly, drenching him in rainbow droplets, then looked meaningfully at him as if to say, 'Well hurry up, throw it again!'

It was scorching hot. I sat down on the upturned boat next to Re and we took off our trainers and socks. Our feet were black with dirt and grime and mine were blistered.

Gingerly, we tiptoed over the grass and stones down to the water's edge. I dipped a toe in and drew back with a big gasp but a little detail like ice-cold water was never going to put Re off.

'Come on, Vicky, don't be such a conkhog! It's lovely and warm.'

'It's freezing!' I squealed. But Rhianna didn't care. She was already paddling merrily in.

'Vicky, let's play Monster Feet!'

I looked over at Daniel who was watching us. I could have died with embarrassment. Monster Feet was a game we used to play in our old paddling pool when Mum was alive.

Basically it consisted of stomping flat-footed in and out of the pool with our arms outstretched, making daft noises. It could last anything from five minutes to an hour depending on Re's enthusiasm. I glanced at her. She was already getting into role, Sumo wrestler style, lurching and swaying from one foot to the other and growling softly.

'Rrrrrrrrrrrrrrrrhhh!'

I sighed. It looked like we were in for a long session . . .

Suddenly Jamie rushed past us. He'd pulled off his T-shirt, socks and trainers and rolled up his jeans. With a loud whoop he crashed into the water, then turned and started splashing us. Re screamed and tried to run away from him.

'Jamie, stop it! Daniel's mum and dad might hear us,' I snapped irritably.

'They've gone out,' said Daniel who called to Jip to come out of the lake.

'Thought they were supposed to be teaching you,' teased Jamie as he got ready to give us another almighty soaking.

'Shut up, Jamie,' I said, looking at Daniel who was glaring coldly at Jamie.

'Shut up yourself,' he retorted, splashing Re and me more furiously.

I'd had enough, what with Re's Monster Feet and now Jamie soaking me there was no longer any point worrying what Daniel thought about me.

'Right, you've asked for it!' I cupped my hands and threw as much water at him as I could. 'Get him, Re!' I yelled and war was declared.

Five minutes later the three of us were soaked through. Rhianna and Jamie continued the fight, laughing and yelling and chasing each other round and round like a couple of puppies. I waded out of the lake and threw myself down on to the ground next to Daniel. Jip lay by his side, wet and smelly, vigorously chewing on his precious stick.

'I haven't even got a towel,' I said with a lame laugh.

Daniel ignored me and continued staring out at the lake.

'Re's . . .' I wanted to explain my sister to him. I searched for the right words. 'She's just kind of young for her age. She doesn't understand stuff.'

'She's OK.'

'Sometimes. Sometimes not.'

'You can't choose your family – just your friends.' He was scowling at Jamie.

'Jamie doesn't mean to be nasty, really he doesn't.'

'Could have fooled me.'

'He's just angry. That's all. Takes things out on other people.'

There was a brief silence. Then Daniel looked at me sheepishly. 'Me too.'

We exchanged a small smile. The ice was broken.

I looked over the shimmering lake at two white swans dipping their black and orange beaks into the silky water, then turning their long graceful necks to preen their feathers.

'Pretty cool here, isn't it?' I said.

I started telling Daniel about the park where Rosie and I would hang out sometimes after school. Rosie called it an oasis of tranquillity but that's just her sense of humour. Some of its more attractive features included broken swings that were roped off but never mended, a rusty old pram floating on the boating lake and colourful graffiti covering the walls of the public loos. I looked out over the lake again as one of the swans stretched its wings and flapped them elegantly. No contest.

'They nested on the island last year,' said Daniel quietly. 'And the year before.'

'Guess they know a good place when they see it . . . Like your cave.'

Daniel smiled. 'Not as comfy as home though.'

Now it was my turn to clam up. Daniel looked at me, his dark brown eyes becoming soft and gentle. I shuffled my feet, slightly embarrassed by his steady gaze.

'We were in care,' I said. 'Can't call that a proper home.'

'S'pose not.'

'Our mum's dead.'

'Sorry.'

'S'OK.' I gave a little laugh to show him it didn't matter. 'She died ages ago.'

I tried to conjure up her face in my mind's eye but it was as if some invisible force was rubbing out the details as fast as I tried to remember them. Shocked, I concentrated harder but all I could see was her small shrunken form, swaddled in blankets, and eased awkwardly into a deck chair next to *Guinevere* where she dozed undisturbed under the pretence of watching us play.

'You all right?' Daniel asked.

'Course.' I pasted on a grin. 'So . . . Is it fun having your parents teach you?'

He shrugged.

'Not bad. Can't get away with "The dog's eaten my

homework" excuse any more though.'

I laughed a bit too loudly and a bit too long. Daniel looked at me. I needed to fill the gap, keep things normal.

'So aren't you s'posed to be, like, having lessons now?'

'Mum and Dad are decorating so I'm actually working hard on my project.'

'What sort of project?'

'Astronomy.'

'Wow . . . I'm a Pisces by the way.'

'That's astrology.'

'Only teasing.'

'I'm Scorpio. Mean, moody and vicious when roused.'

'Really?'

'No. I'm a wimp.'

'You don't seem like a wimp. And I've met a few.'

'Ta. But take it from me. I'm wimp to the core.' There was a sudden edginess in his voice. Somewhere along the line the joke had disappeared and he was deadly serious. He seemed to realise and gave a small laugh.

'Sorry. Told you I was mean and moody. So what about your dad?'

The last thing I wanted to talk about was Dad so I started to trot out the old story about him being abroad. Daniel was still looking at me and I could feel my face blushing beetroot. I knew he didn't believe me.

'If my kids needed me, I'd be back like a shot,' he said quietly.

'Well maybe our dad doesn't care about us,' I retorted with just a bit too much emotion in my voice.

'So you're running away from him too?'

There was an awkward silence. Daniel was watching Re and Jamie in the lake. I felt the anger bubbling up in me. Just who did this kid think he was?

'He's in prison, if you must know.'

It felt good to blurt out those words. It was like a huge weight coming off me. Then before I could stop myself, everything came tumbling out about Dad's drinking and Mr McCready's special deliveries.

Before I knew it, I was telling him how Dad got arrested. I'd never told anyone before. It happened a few weeks after we were taken into care. When he came to visit us, I'd noticed he looked more and more dishevelled each time, like he'd given up or something. The last time he came he'd been drinking. A lot. I could smell it on his breath and tell by the way he slurred his words and kept repeating the same thing he'd said a few minutes before. Then the visits stopped. A week later, Mrs Frankish spared a minute out of her busy schedule and filled me in with a quick phone call. The police had stopped Dad on the motorway. They said he'd been swerving from lane to lane so they'd breathalysed him and found he was well over the limit. When they looked in the van he was driving, they found it was full of stolen tellies. To cut a long story short, they arrested him, he went to court and was sent to prison.

Jamie and Re came running out of the water, and I clammed up again. Daniel didn't say anything but he'd noticed I'd stopped talking. Those eyes didn't miss much.

'We're going to swim to the island,' said Jamie. 'You coming?'

'Jamie be careful —'

'Vicky, don't be such a chicken. Just because you can't swim,' Jamie taunted.

'I can . . . A bit.' I looked at Daniel and could feel my face reddening again.

'I'll stay here with you,' he said.

'Can't you swim either?' asked Re bluntly.

'Yeah, I can swim.' I detected that cold note in Daniel's voice again. 'I just don't want to, that's all.'

'I bet you can't really,' Jamie teased.

'Jamie!' I hissed, glancing at Daniel.

Daniel was glaring at Jamie. A hard glint came into his eyes. Mean, moody and vicious when roused.

'Bet you're scared like Vicky.' Jamie started making chicken noises. 'Bet you're just saying you can. That's what she does.'

'OK, I'll prove it.' Daniel kicked off his trainers. He pulled off his T-shirt and stood in front of us. I just managed to hide a gasp. Covering most of his chest and stomach was an ugly, dark purple blotch. The skin looked sore and angry.

'Come on then,' said Daniel, staring coldly at Jamie. 'I'll race you to the island and back.'

I looked at Jamie. He was fidgeting nervously, trying not to look at Daniel's torso but unable to stop himself. Re just stared unashamedly, her mouth open wide as Daniel turned and walked down to the water.

'It's OK,' he snapped. 'It's not contagious.'

chapter 27

Daniel was a much better swimmer than Jamie. He beat
the pants off him. By miles and miles. He beat me too
but only just. Vicky stood at the edge of the lake but she
didn't cheer us on. When we came out Vicky made us
dry ourselves with Jamie's sweatshirt. Then we all sat on
the boat looking at the island and eating cheese rolls. I
had three and I was still starving. Jamie didn't say anything. Nobody said anything. It was getting really boring
all sitting around saying nothing so I thought maybe I
should say something.

'Daniel what's that big purple splodge on your tummy?'
Vicky pulled a funny face and said, 'Re . . .'
But I wanted to know. 'Does it come off, like felt pen?'
'No.'
'So what is it?'

'When I was nine I tipped a saucepan of boiling water over me.'

'Does it still hurt?' I asked.

'Only here.' He pointed to his head. I didn't understand. 'Why?'

'Re drop it.' Vicky got up off the boat.

'Why Daniel?'

'At school they called me Lurgy Boy. One girl refused to swim in the school pool with me and got her parents to complain.'

'You should have just whacked her one,' said Jamie.

Daniel ignored him.

'Is that why you don't go to school?' Vicky asked.

'What do you think?' He quickly pulled on his T-shirt even though he was still wet. 'We all run away from stuff we can't handle,' he said, looking straight at Vicky who went bright red.

'But what about your mates?' said Jamie.

'What mates? I was different. You know how it is. No one likes different.' He got up. 'And I was really stupid to think you lot wouldn't be the same.'

I thought about my friend Maxine. There wasn't anyone like her.

'I like different,' I said, picking up the last cheese roll and taking a big bite.

But Daniel wasn't listening. He'd already snatched up his jumper and was marching off through the woods with Jip at his side.

chapter 28

We didn't stay long at the lake. The sun disappeared behind clouds and it felt chilly. Jamie didn't feel like swimming again and Re just kept asking why Daniel didn't like us any more. In the end, when we were more or less dry, we started walking back through the woods in silence. Rhianna stuck close to me and jumped a mile every time she heard a sound.

'There's nothing to be scared of, Re.'

'That's what you think,' she replied, looking round nervously. We must have taken a wrong path because we found ourselves near a narrow lane. Jamie spotted something lying by the kerbside and wanted to go over to investigate.

'Better not,' I said, turning back the way we came, 'someone might see us.'

'Don't be daft, Vicky, there's no one around.' He ran off before I could stop him.

It was a rabbit. I thought it was dead at first because it wasn't moving but when we looked more closely we saw it was trembling slightly. Its eyes were wide open and staring.

'Must have been hit by a car or something,' said Jamie. Re stroked the soft grey fur. The rabbit barely flinched.

'Let's take it back to the cave and look after it,' said Re, gently picking it up.

I looked at the little bundle cradled in Re's big clumsy hands and couldn't help thinking that things didn't look very promising.

'Please, Vicky.'

'I don't know . . .'

Jamie's caterpillar eyebrows knitted together in an anxious scowl.

'You wouldn't like to be left on the road to be squashed, would you?' he said.

Re joined in. 'You wouldn't, Vicky.'

I was definitely outnumbered. 'All right.' Suddenly I was aware of a deep rumbling noise down the lane. And it was growing louder. 'Something's coming!' I hissed.

We dived for cover behind the hedge just as a coach turned the corner and pulled up about ten metres ahead of us. It was a battered old school bus. There were some kids play fighting on the back seats but no one saw us. The door swished open and we could hear the racket inside. After a second or two, a shaven-headed boy of about fifteen tumbled out, followed closely by a girl with eyes like little black beads stuck in her pale face. The girl yelled something rude at the driver as the door of the bus swished shut. The boy laughed and the pair sauntered off down the lane taking swipes at each other with their school bags, cheering when they scored a direct hit.

We waited till they were out of sight then turned back into the woods.

'So much for not seeing anyone,' I said.

There was a small village about a mile away from Great Auntie Irene's house. This road must lead there, I thought. Dad and Great Auntie Irene had walked us there once but Mum had stayed at the house, too tired to join us. We'd bought sweets from the little shop and posted some cards to our friends. It was run by a lady in a flowery apron and sold everything you could possibly think of. It was like an Aladdin's cave because you never knew what you'd find sitting in a dusty corner. On one of the back shelves, wedged between balls of fluorescent-coloured wool and a box of garden trowels, there was a row of large glass jars full of all sorts of sweets we'd never even heard of before. We were each allowed a little paper bagful − tangy cola cubes, chewy milk bottles, rhubarb and custards with sugar on the rhubarb side and liquorice comfits that stained your tongue black as you ate them. What I'd give for a bag of those sweets now, I thought.

We found our way back to our cave. Jamie went straight in, took the old biscuit tin down from the shelf and pulled it open. He lined it with his T-shirt before taking the rabbit gently from Re and placing it inside. He took his drink flask, poured a little water over his finger and put it in front of the rabbit's mouth. It didn't move. It just sat in the tin, staring straight ahead, helplessly.

'Can I hold him again?' asked Re.

Jamie passed the tin to her. She sat transfixed by the rabbit on her lap, hardly daring to move in case she frightened it.

I checked our supplies. We were down to some orange juice and a few potatoes.

'We could bake them in a camp fire,' said Jamie hopefully.

'We haven't got any matches.'

'Who needs matches?' retorted Jamie, taking his camping book down from the shelf.

It was written by a man called Falcon B. Tremaine and had his picture on the back cover. He had a big fuzzy beard and wore a bush hat with a feather in the headband. He looked pretty tough except for the white socks he wore under his sandals. Jamie flicked through the pages until he got to the chapter about fire lighting. Concentrating hard, he slowly started reading. About ten minutes later he looked up at us, his face like thunder.

'Stupid book!' he muttered, throwing it across the cave and stomping out, swearing under his breath.

'What's the matter?' asked Re.

I picked up the book and turned to the pages he'd been reading. There was a whole page on how to cut a square of turf from the ground and six detailed diagrams showing different ways of laying the twigs and kindling. I finally got to the crucial sentence.

'*Strike the match close to the kindling and let it burn halfway down before applying it.*'

I quickly turned the pages looking for how to light a fire without matches. Nothing.

'We don't have any matches, you stupid fuzzball!' I yelled at the photo on the back cover.

'I'm hungry, Vicky,' Re said, stroking the rabbit. 'And I want to see Daniel.'

'Come on,' I said. 'Let's go and find him and try and make up.'

Jamie didn't want to come at first but he tagged along once Re and I set off. We made our way up the path to the end of Daniel's garden and saw him on the patio outside the back door brushing Jip's coat.

I exchanged grins with Re. He had his head down and he hadn't seen us yet. We were just about to climb over the gate when the back door swung open. I pulled Re back and we all hid behind the fence. His mum appeared and said something to him. He nodded then gave Jip one last brush before disappearing inside.

'What do we do now?' asked Re.

I shrugged in reply.

But things were soon taken out of our hands. A few minutes later the back door opened again and Daniel and both his mum and dad emerged. His dad was carrying a bulky-looking holdall and Daniel had a rucksack on his back. His mum locked the back door.

'Are they going away?' asked Re.

'I don't know.'

Daniel called to Jip and they all disappeared round the side of the house. We heard the sounds of car doors slamming and then the starting of an engine.

We caught glimpses of the red car as it drove away up the lane. It was only then that the awful reality of our situation suddenly hit me. Daniel was our lifeline. Without his help, we were stuck.

Chapter 29

When we got back to the cave, Vicky said that there wasn't anything for tea. Jamie wanted to eat the potatoes raw but Vicky said raw potatoes were poisonous. Jamie didn't believe her and when she wasn't looking he took a big bite out of one. As he chewed it he made a face. Then he spat it out on the ground.

'Let's go to the shop and buy some stuff,' said Jamie.

'Yeah, come on!'

But as usual Vicky was being a pain.

'No way. We can't risk it. They're looking for us. We all turn up at the shop and that's it. Game over.'

'We could dress up so no one knows it's us,' I said.

'What as – the three little pigs?' said Jamie.

'Jamie's got his spiderman suit.'

'Back home. And it's "age five". It doesn't fit any more.'

'Look, we're not dressing up, OK Re? One, we've got nothing to dress up in, two, we'd look really stupid and three, everyone would notice us straight away.'

'Well I think it's a good plan.'

'Trust me, it's not.' Vicky went out of the cave and Jamie turned to me.

'Come on. I've got an idea.'

'What?'

'Let's go and find some roots and berries,' he whispered.

'What for?'

'To eat of course. That's what they always do in survival stories and stuff.'

'OK,' I said.

'But don't tell Vicky.'

'Why not?'

'Because she'll stop us. You know her.'

'Yeah. Always fussing.'

'Anyway . . . she wouldn't know a root if it was hanging off her nose,' said Jamie with a giggle.

I gently put the tin down in a corner of the cave. I tucked Jamie's T-shirt over the rabbit so he wouldn't be cold and put my little penguin next to him so he wouldn't be lonely, then we went out. Vicky was sitting outside. She asked where we were going.

'Nowhere,' said Jamie.

'Don't go far.'

'We won't.'

'It'll be dark soon. Stay together!'

We followed the stream for a bit and then started looking

for berries. I don't know where they all were but we couldn't find any. We were just going to give up when I saw some green ones. Jamie thought they were blackberries but they weren't ripe. There weren't any other berries so I said to Jamie we'd better just get some nice roots. Jamie said good idea and started digging at the ground with his hands. They got covered in brown mud but he kept digging and digging one hole then another one and another. Then he pulled something up. It looked like a big hairy worm.

'I'm not eating worms Jamie.' Ollie Stanmore ate a worm once for a dare and then he was sick over Charlene Slackton's new shoes. They had peepholes and it all squelched out over her toes. It made me feel yucky just thinking about it.

'It's not a worm, it's a root.'

'Oh.'

He put it to his nose and sniffed it.

'What does it smell like?' I asked.

Jamie shrugged and put it under my nose.

'Eurgh! Smells like a worm!'

'It's not a worm, all right? It's not a worm! It's a flipping root!'

I watched him sniff it again. He made a face then threw it back on the ground.

'Aren't you going to eat it?' I asked.

'No.'

I'm glad. Being sick is horrible. Especially when bits of chewed up worm come down your nose.

'Let's just get some leaves instead,' I said.

Jamie picked a couple off a tree and we nibbled one each but they were disgusting. We spat them out. It was getting dark and Jamie was cross.

'If we could have lit a fire we could have cooked a wild pig or something,' he said.

'Where would we get a wild pig?' I asked.

'I don't know – here in the woods . . .'

'But we can't even find any berries.'

'Shut up Re.'

'I'm hungry!' I told him.

'So am I!'

'But you said we'd get something to eat. You said —'

'Shut up!' he shouted really crossly.

'But —'

'Shut up, just shut up or I'll . . . I'll cook your stupid rabbit.'

I looked at him. 'You wouldn't dare!'

'I would. Yum yum . . . Rabbit stew, here we come . . .'

He laughed really nastily and turned round to go. I pushed past him and started running. I had to get back to the cave before him and make sure he didn't touch Peter.

Chapter 30

It was getting dark when Jamie came back. I was furious.

'I said don't go far! Where the hell have you been? And where's Re?'

Jamie shrugged.

'She ran on. She should have been back ages before me.'

'You let her go off by herself?'

He wouldn't look me in the eye. I caught hold of him but he twisted away from me. 'I can't help it if she runs off, can I?' he shouted.

'Jamie – you know she doesn't go anywhere on her own. You know that. We have to look after her – she can't look after herself.'

Jamie looked uncomfortable. I ran into the cave and grabbed his torch from the shelf, glancing at the rabbit.

It was still curled up in the tin next to the little penguin ornament. I could see its ribs faintly moving as it laboured to breathe. I didn't need to be a vet to know things looked pretty pear-shaped.

Outside the cave, Jamie was scuffing the dirt with the toe of his trainer. He looked upset.

'I'm going to find her,' I said.

'I want to come with you.'

'No. You've got to stay here. If she does manage to find her way back, she'll wonder where we are.'

I turned on the torch. Its faint beam lit up a tiny circle of ground. Jamie pulled a face.

'The batteries are run down. I let Re play with it.'

I quickly turned it off, thinking I might need it more later. I glanced around me. The woods looked different in the dimming light. Unfriendly and unwelcoming. I set off alongside the stream half wishing I'd asked Jamie to come with me.

Then I thought of Re and I felt sick. I didn't like the dark much, but ever since Mum died Re had been absolutely petrified of it. I had to find her quickly.

I scoured the woods calling out her name. There was no reply, only the rustling of leaves and the snuffling of what I hoped and kept telling myself were just cute little woodland animals. Once or twice I allowed myself to get spooked and swung round, terrified and convinced there was someone or something following me. Then in the distance I heard the faint whine of motorbikes. Thinking I must be nearer the road than I realised, I turned away from the noise but must have misjudged where it was coming from as the whine became louder and more insistent and grew into a roar. It was then I saw Jamie about ten metres behind. The little tyke had followed me. I was furious and about to lay into him when, through the darkness, two separate headlights beamed around the woods illuminating trees and bushes. I motioned angrily to Jamie to hide and we both ducked down low so whoever they were wouldn't see us. Two dirt bikes threaded their way through the trees, revving as they mounted each slope and screeching down the other side. I knew Jamie would have been impressed and just prayed that he had enough sense to keep his head down. We couldn't afford to be spotted by anyone. I watched the riders weave their way into the distance. At one point, one of them tried to swerve round a bush but he misjudged the angle and nearly came off the bike, swearing noisily as he got his balance back and revved off. At last they were gone, the whining sound slowly faded and I got up from my hiding place. Without their headlights it was frighteningly dark. I called softly to Jamie and he emerged from the shadows. He was soaking wet.

'Couldn't you have found a dry place to hide?' I hissed angrily.

'I couldn't help it . . . I slipped over.' He was shivering and his teeth chattered uncontrollably.

'I told you to stay at the cave.'

'I was worried about Re. It was my fault she ran off.'

His grimy face was streaked with the tracks of his tears. I softened.

'Come on. We'll find her.'

I turned on the torch. Its faint beam was pathetic but it was all we had.

Chapter 31

It was too dark. And everything looked different. The cave wasn't where it was before so I didn't know which way to go. I wanted Vicky but I was too scared to shout for her in case they heard me. You know who I mean. The things with sharp teeth and claws, the things that come out from their hiding places just when you're on your own and suck out your insides before you even see them. The shadow things. I knew they were waiting. Hiding. They like the dark. They want you to think they're not there because you can't see them. But I knew just where they were. They were behind the trees. When the branches tap on your window in the middle of the night. That's them. They used to tap on the window outside Mum's room at the hospital but I always asked one of the nurses to leave the light on all the way through the night. Maybe one night they forgot so that was why Mum wasn't there in the morning. Maybe it was the shadow things that took her away.

I didn't want to think about this so I kept walking really quietly. Then through the trees I saw some really bright lights moving about and it suddenly got noisy. The monsters were coming to get me! The lights got nearer and nearer and then I saw it wasn't shadow monsters at all, it was people on motorbikes. It was too late to run off. One of them shouted at me and pointed and then they both started riding their bikes round and round me in a circle like they were playing a game. I didn't like it. They didn't have helmets on so I could see their faces. It was the boy and girl that got off the bus. They rode their bikes closer and closer. I was scared they were going to run me over.

I told them to go away but they didn't take any notice. The girl looked at the boy then turned round and with a nasty smile started to drive her bike straight at me. I shut my eyes and felt her whoosh past. The boy followed. The front of his bike scraped against my legs and I fell over backwards into the mud. They both laughed. I got up and ran. They chased after me for a bit but then I tripped over a big sticking-out tree root and fell on the ground again. Now I started yelling and yelling as loud as I could. I didn't care any more if the shadow monsters heard me or not.

Chapter 32

We heard Rhianna's shouts and found her cowering in a ditch between some tree roots, crying uncontrollably.

'Re! Are you OK?' I asked as Jamie pulled her to her feet.

'I told them to stop but they wouldn't. They wouldn't stop!'

I put my arms round her and hugged her tightly. Gradually the sobbing slowed to a few random hiccups. She grew calm and we helped her brush the mud from her clothes and hair.

'It's all right now. They've gone. Let's get back to the cave. We'll be safe there.'

We started to retrace our steps, but it was harder than I thought and we seemed to be going round and round in circles. It was more by luck than judgement that we eventually found our way back. After seeing the same fallen tree for the second time, I was just beginning to give up when I spotted a stream. With our fingers crossed that it was ours, we started to follow it. We were lucky. It was our stream and it led us all the way back to the cave. Jamie was quiet as he pulled off his wet clothes and crawled into his sleeping bag.

'I'm sorry, Vicky,' he muttered as he snuggled down inside.

I heard a muffled sob from his direction and saw him turn his head away from me. I remembered he was only a kid.

'It's all right. Forget it now.'

'But what are we going to do? We haven't got anything to eat. We've got to eat.'

'Go to sleep now. Things'll look better in the morning.'

I slept really badly that night. I had dream after dream about food. Plates of bangers and mash, school dinner sponge and custard, piles of cakes and biscuits – lovely, luscious, delicious food but always out of reach, either on the other side of a ravine or suspended over a pit of snakes or guarded by a pack of vicious wolves. I was just about to get my hands on a huge double cheese and pineapple pizza when I woke to find Rhianna shaking me. I looked out of the cave entrance and saw it was morning already. Jamie was awake too and the pair of them were staring down at me as if I had the power to produce a full-blown fry-up from inside my sleeping bag.

'I'm starving. And so is Peter.' She thrust the rabbit under my nose. Its eyes were glazed and its nostrils caked with brown gunk. Food was probably the last thing on its mind. I looked at Re and Jamie, expecting, depending on me to do something. But what? I thought about Daniel. What if he had gone away for a few days? He and his parents had left carrying a holdall and rucksack. And they'd taken Jip. Even if Daniel was back now, he'd been really angry with us yesterday. What if he didn't want anything more to do with us? I sighed.

'OK. We'll go to the shop. But we're going to have to be very, very careful.'

I reached over and found my purse. Hopefully, I emptied the contents on to my sleeping bag. My heart sank. We had precisely fifty-five pence. At least we could buy some matches so we could light a fire and cook the last few potatoes.

We reached the village just as the shop was opening up. We hid behind the old village hall with its painted corrugated iron walls and watched as the lady in the flowery apron darted in and out, carrying boxes of fruit and veg which she placed on a slatted bench in front of the window. As she worked, she greeted people as they passed and still managed to keep up a monologue to someone inside.

'Alf, these carrots are on the turn! Morning, Mrs Gratton – not looking so good today, is it? Alf, bring me out some of those bananas, would you? Still, if we get a bit of rain it'll do the garden good, won't it? They're in the back storeroom! Mr Gratton all right, is he? Nasty thing arthritis. My mother suffered terrible. That knitting pattern's in . . .'

It was now or never. I turned to Jamie and Re.

'Wait here,' I told them.

'But I want to come too,' pleaded Re.

'No. Stay here with Jamie.'

'Please!'

'People are looking for three runaway kids. Our pictures have been on the telly and in the papers. If I'm on my own, there's less chance I'll be recognised.'

'But what if you get caught?'

I hesitated before I replied, hoping neither of them detected the worry hiding in my voice.

'I won't. Now stay out of sight. I'll be back in a minute.'

I smoothed down my matted hair, brushed a patch of dried mud off my jeans then took a deep breath and started walking as calmly as I could towards the shop. I knew I had to behave as normally as possible but felt as if there was a hammer banging away in my chest that could be heard a mile away.

'Morning, dear . . .'

'Hello,' my voice wobbled. I pushed the corners of my mouth up into a smile as I tried to stop myself shaking. I quickly walked past her and into the shop.

'Be with you in a moment,' she called after me.

The shop was empty. No sign of Alf. Near the door was a wire stand with fresh loaves of bread, cakes and sausage rolls sitting on white doilies. The smallest loaf cost eighty pence. As I looked at it hungrily, my stomach gave out a huge rumble in sympathy. The delicious smell of fresh baked bread filled the tiny room. I stared at the golden bumpy crust just waiting to be torn apart to reveal the soft white inside, and my mouth watered like it had never watered before.

Peeping through the door, I saw the woman with her back to me, chatting nineteen to the dozen with someone. I knew it was wrong but we needed food to survive. We were desperate. I reached out, snatched the loaf and tucked it under my arm. There were three sausage rolls on the rack underneath. I grabbed them too and stuffed them in my jacket pocket. Unable to stop myself, I wheeled round and filled my other pocket with several bars of chocolate. Then I shoved a packet of biscuits and a tin of ham down inside my jacket, bracing my arm across my stomach to stop anything falling out. I was about to take a block of cheese when the woman bustled back in. I froze in panic, my face burning. I felt sick as I looked down at my scruffy clothes bulging with the things I'd stolen.

'Now then. Just the loaf was it, dear?' she asked.

She hadn't noticed. I had to stay cool.

'Um . . . and a box of matches, please.'

She turned momentarily to take down the matches from a high shelf. This was my chance. All I had to do was run past her out of the door and I'd be safe. For what seemed like an eternity but must have been only a nightmare split second, I hesitated, my feet rooted to the spot. The moment was lost as she swung round, blocking the shop doorway behind her. I was trapped.

'On holiday, are you dear?' she said pleasantly as she handed me the matches.

I nodded dumbly, acutely aware of my bedraggled

appearance and desperately praying she wouldn't notice my bulging pockets. The packet of biscuits had worked its way round to my hip and was threatening to slip out from under my jacket at any moment. I tried to edge it back up with my elbow.

The shop door opened. Someone else was coming in. I didn't dare look. It was probably Alf. There were now two of them to catch me. I wouldn't stand a chance. Another second and they'd put two and two together and realise something wasn't right. Another two seconds and my stash would come slipping out from under my jacket and cascade on to the floor. Angrily, they'd bar the door, Alf would call the police, they'd arrive in a flash, Re and Jamie would be rounded up and we'd all be sent back in disgrace to Mrs Frankish who would frostily dispatch us to wherever she felt fit without a qualm. This was it. The end of our journey. The end of us as a family.

'Lovely part of the world, isn't it? Wouldn't live any-where else if you paid me,' the woman was saying. 'That's one pound and five pence, please.'

Sweating and playing for time, I fumbled in my half empty purse then gave all the money I had to the woman.

'Ooh. There's only fifty-five pence here.'

'Think you might have dropped this outside,' said a voice from behind me. I swung round. It was Daniel. He was holding out a fifty pence piece. I had never been more glad to see anyone in my whole life.

'Oh yes . . . Thank you.'

He handed it to the woman who was now staring at me oddly.

I didn't wait for her response. Red-faced with shame, I quickly scurried past them to the door and ran out across the road and round the back of the village hall where Jamie and Re were waiting.

'What's up, Vick?' asked Jamie when he saw my face.

I shook my head. I couldn't speak. If I'd have tried to say anything I knew I would have burst into tears there and then.

Chapter 33

Daniel came out of the shop a little bit after Vicky. I waved to him. He stopped, looked round then walked over to us. I gave him a big hug.

'We thought you'd gone away!' I said.

'I went over to my gran's for the night. We got home about half an hour ago.'

'Come back with us to the cave, Daniel, I want to show you Peter.'

'Who's Peter?'

'My rabbit.'

I asked Vicky if it was all right and Daniel could come with us. She didn't say anything. She just nodded.

'We can all be friends again,' I told her.

She still didn't say anything.

'Don't you like Daniel any more?' I asked her.

'It's not that,' she said, kicking the ground.

'Didn't you get any food?' I asked.

'Yeah I got some.'

She wouldn't tell me what she got. She was in a right moody. I don't know why. Jamie wasn't talking to Daniel either, so I walked with him and told him all about Peter.

Daniel said he'd show us a short cut. As we walked past an old church we saw two dirt bikes on the ground.

Then we saw them. They were sitting on the steps at the back, smoking and laughing.

'It's them from last night,' I said, moving closer to Vicky.

Daniel was worried too. He looked round as if he wanted to run away. The girl looked up and stared straight at him.

'Hey, it's Lurgy Boy!' she shouted. She threw her cigarette on to the grass. 'How's your lurgy, Lurgy Boy?'

She laughed and turned to the boy. He nodded back at her. Then they got up and started walking over to us.

'Who are your saddo new friends, Lurgy Boy?'

The girl stared at me. I tried to hide behind Vicky.

'Hey, it's that retard from last night – you want to watch where you're going if you don't want to get run over . . . Retard.'

Jamie looked really angry – he was ready to whack them both. Vicky caught his arm and pulled him back.

'Let's just walk the other way,' whispered Daniel, turning round.

'You're not running back to Mummy today, Lurgy Boy. You stay right where you are!'

Daniel started to turn away.

'I said stay, Lurgy Boy!'

Daniel stayed. He looked very small. The bullies went up to him.

'Now then, what are you Lurgy Boy?' said the girl. 'Tell these saddos what you are.'

'He's our friend,' I said to the girl. 'Stop teasing him!'

'Stay out of this retard,' said the girl, spinning round to me.

Daniel stepped forward. 'Leave her alone,' he shouted in a wobbly voice. 'She hasn't done anything.'

'Ooooh . . . Come over all brave, have we now? That's new. I wonder what's got into Lurgy Boy?'

'I'll find out,' said the boy. He leapt on Daniel's back and locked his arms round his neck. Daniel struggled with him but the boy was much bigger and stronger. Daniel started making coughing noises.

'Nope! Same old Lurgy Boy!'

'Stop it!' Vicky shouted.

With a roar Jamie ran forward, grabbed the boy and ripped him off Daniel. The boy yelled. He thumped on to the ground. Jamie dived on to him and sat on him so he couldn't get up. He was much smaller than the boy but he was really really angry now. When Jamie gets angry you don't want to mess with him. Really you don't. He pushed his face close up to the boy's. His caterpillar eyebrows were nearly touching him.

'Don't you ever pick on him or my sister or anyone, ever again!' said Jamie.

The boy looked scared now. 'He's hurting me! Get him off!' he wailed. He started wriggling and kicking his legs around trying to get away from Jamie. The girl grabbed at Jamie's hair with her hands and started pulling it.

Now Daniel tried to pull her off Jamie but she punched him away like he was a little fly. Jamie shouted at her but she carried on. He swizzed round and was going to hit her but suddenly the boy kicked her right on the nose. I don't think he meant to do that. She let go of Jamie's hair. A trickle of red dribbled down on to her white top.

'You idiot! This is brand new!' she screamed at the boy. She whacked him over the head.

'Wasn't my fault!' he whined. He rubbed his short spiky hair with his dirty hand.

'Come on!' said Vicky. She grabbed my arm. We all started running.

'We'll get you back . . . We will . . . Just you wait!' the girl shouted at us as she rubbed blood and snot across her face.

Chapter 34

Once out of the village, we scrambled through the woods, along the stream and back to safety.

We were almost back at the cave when Daniel turned to Jamie. 'Thanks,' he said quietly.

Jamie suppressed a grin. 'Any time,' he muttered as he pretended to re-tie his trainer lace.

Boys are such uncomplicated creatures; this was all that was needed for them to be friends again.

Re grabbed the loaf of bread from under my arm. 'Come on. I'm starving.'

Daniel opened his rucksack and took out a big plastic bottle of milk, a jar of peanut butter, a bunch of bananas and a huge bar of chocolate. 'Bought it to go with the bread,' he said with a smile.

I hurried into the cave and started unloading my stolen

stash of food on to the shelf, too ashamed to tell the others what I'd done. I didn't hear Daniel come in and, turning round, dropped the handful of chocolate bars in surprise.

He looked at me, puzzled.

'Thought you didn't have any food . . .'

Ashamed, I started scrabbling on the floor, picking them up. I indicated the rest of the food on the shelf.

'I stole it all from the shop this morning,' I mumbled, hanging my head and waiting for his reaction. 'I'm a thief.'

He didn't say anything for a moment.

'You were only trying to look after Jamie and Re.'

'But up till today I've never stolen anything in my whole life.'

Suddenly I thought of Dad. How did he feel when he was delivering all those stolen tellies? Gramps, his dad, had been a policeman. As a boy, Dad had been brought up very strictly, and that strong moral sense had stayed with him.

'Dad always used to tell us it was important to do the right thing. Not to tell lies. Not to cheat – even at Monopoly. Not to take biscuits from the tin without asking. But then he goes and does a whopping great wrong thing himself. He knew full well it was wrong but he'd carried on doing it again and again until he was caught.'

'He must have been totally desperate,' said Daniel. 'Just like you were.'

I felt the tears prickling in my eyes and screwed them up to force them back.

Daniel didn't say a word. He just wrapped his arms round me and hugged me. I felt calmer. I looked up at him.

'Thanks for what you did this morning. You were really brave,' I said.

'You're joking, aren't you?'

'Not at all. First, in the shop you saved my skin, then when that horrible girl started on Rhianna . . .'

'I didn't do much though, did I? If it hadn't have been for Jamie —'

'Oh, Jamie's always fighting. It's like it's his hobby or something. You were really scared but you still spoke up.'

Daniel smiled at me.

'I couldn't sleep last night,' he said. 'I thought you were really angry with me, for throwing that stupid wobbly and leaving you at the lake yesterday. I thought I'd blown it and you wouldn't want anything more to do with me.' He glanced at me then added quickly, 'You and Re and Jamie, I mean.'

'Don't be daft,' I said, thinking how nice his eyes were when he smiled. 'I . . . We all really like you.'

Re came running into the cave. She saw Daniel's arms around me and did a double take.

'What's wrong?' she asked.

'Nothing,' Daniel and I said at exactly the same time.

'Then why are you hugging?'

Daniel and I immediately stepped away from each other. I caught his eye and we both smiled.

'Because we're all friends again,' he said with a shrug.

Breakfast was like a feast. A celebration. Maybe it was the food or maybe it was just the fact we were all together, but everyone was in a good mood. Jamie and Re had made peanut butter, banana and chocolate sandwiches and we washed them down with the cool fresh milk. Daniel wouldn't have any. He said he'd had a huge fry-up for breakfast and happily watched as we demolished the whole lot between us. We joked and laughed about all sorts of silly stuff, like furnishing the cave with a few luxuries – maybe a DVD player and telly run off solar panels, a fancy barbecue to cook hot meals and a hot chocolate drink dispenser with marshmallows, whipped cream and sprinkles as standard. We fantasised how we could happily live undiscovered at the cave for years. Finally, one day we'd come out of hiding like a bunch of Rip Van Winkles and surprise everyone by our re-appearance.

When we'd finished every single crumb, we lolled back on the grass. Re carefully showed Daniel the tin containing the rabbit. He was hunched down even more on Jamie's T-shirt.

'I'm only keeping him till he's better,' she told him, 'then I'm going to let him free, because he's a wild rabbit not a house one.'

I watched as Daniel gently stroked the rabbit's back then darted me a knowing glance.

'He's lovely and soft,' he told Re.

It was late morning by now and despite what the lady in the shop had said, it was turning into another beautiful day. We decided to go down to the lake. Jamie and Re wanted to go for a swim and I said I'd paddle. It was getting hot and the thought of cooling off in the clear water was irresistible.

Daniel said he'd come with us and we made our way through the trees laughing and joking in the warm sunshine as if we didn't have a care in the world.

We came to an abrupt halt as we reached the edge of the woods. Looking down towards the lake, Rhianna blurted out what I was thinking.

'What if those bullies are down there waiting for us?' she asked fearfully.

'I'm not scared of them,' Jamie replied with a scowl. But we still hid behind trees while he and Daniel checked out the shoreline. The place was deserted. Jamie beckoned to us and we joined him and Daniel at the water's edge. The water looked deliciously cool and inviting.

'Hey, Daniel, you coming?' Jamie called as he waded in.

Daniel hesitated for a second. Then he quickly pulled off his T-shirt, revealing the angry scarring on his stomach and chest. This time Jamie didn't bat an eyelid.

'Bet you can't do handstands . . .' he called.

'Bet I can!' retorted Daniel with a grin, charging into the water. They spent ages larking and splashing about.

I kept an eye on the woods, aware that someone might hear us or arrive at any second. Was this how it was going to be, I wondered. Always watching our backs to avoid being discovered? Running from place to place? Living hand to mouth? Lying? Stealing? Hiding? What sort of future was that? The idea of living in our cave for as long as we wanted now seemed totally ridiculous. A little kid's fantasy, I thought flatly.

Chapter 35

Daniel showed me how to do handstands. They're easy-peasy chocolate squeezy. You just dive under the water, plonk your hands on the squelchy weeds at the bottom and kick your legs up at the same time. But don't swallow any water. It tastes of mud. We practised for ages. Vicky just sat on the grass with her arms hugging her knees, looking round behind her at the woods or down at her feet.

'Vicky watch me!'

I did my best handstand so far. She said it was really good but she wasn't even looking.

'You didn't see it!'

'I did . . . It was great.' Her voice sounded funny and she still didn't look up.

'Come in with us!' Jamie called but she just shook her

head. She looked very small scrunched up like that.

Daniel stopped and stared over at her. It was his go but he waded out and went and sat down next to her on the grass. I don't think she saw him because she still didn't look up. He put his arm round her. She didn't push him away, she just leaned on him and looked sad. I suppose she really wanted to do handstands like us. It's not very nice when you can't do things and everyone else can.

Jamie and I carried on for a bit. Jamie wanted to do cart-wheels but they're really hard so we did back-flips instead. They're handstands but you go over and swoosh up through the water in a circle. We did thirty-seven each.

When we came out of the water Daniel and Vicky were still sitting together talking.

'Don't be upset Vicky. I can show you how to do hand-stands tomorrow – I'll hold your legs up for you.'

'Thanks Re,' she said with a small smile.

Daniel grinned at her and then do you know, she went all red and toothy just like she used to with Manky Matt.

Jamie didn't say anything. He was staring out over the lake. Suddenly he turned to us.

'Look!' he said, pointing at the road across the water.

Vicky went white and Daniel jumped up like he had ants in his pants. I don't know what they were making such a fuss about. It was just two police cars driving along.

Chapter 36

'They're coming round this side!' shouted Daniel.

'What are we going to do?'

'They might not be after us . . . It might just be a coincidence . . .' But no one was listening to me and a horrible feeling in the pit of my stomach told me that something was wrong. I remembered the odd expression of the woman in the shop – after I'd gone she must have noticed stuff had been taken, put two and two together and realised who I was.

Daniel had taken Re's hand and had already started running.

'Back to the cave,' he yelled. 'It's your only chance!'

Jamie was hot on their heels. Quickly, I collected up our things and ran full pelt after them.

We reached the cave, panting and breathless. Re was crying, not sure what was going on. I took her inside and tried to calm her down while Jamie and Daniel worked furiously to remove any traces that betrayed our presence.

We heard voices.

'Jamie!' I hissed.

'Get inside!' called Daniel urgently to Jamie, then pulled brambles and wild roses over the mouth of the cave. 'And don't make a sound!'

'I want Baby Emma!'

I peered out through the tangle of stems and leaves. Perched on a bush, Baby Emma and her wardrobe of clothes were sprawled in full view of anyone who passed.

The voices were getting louder.

'They're coming!'

'They'll be here any second!'

'But I want Baby Emma!' wailed Re, her sobs becoming louder and more uncontrollable.

Jamie looked at me. He was thinking exactly what I was thinking. Springing into action, he pushed his way out of the cave, grabbed the doll and the clothes and sprinted back inside. Pulling the brambles back into place, he threw himself down on to the floor next to us and we huddled together hardly daring to breathe.

'Hey, you there!' a man's voice called. 'Stay where you are please.'

We heard them scramble down the slope. There must have been three or four of them. One of them slipped and swore noisily. The first man asked Daniel his name and address and if he'd seen any new kids around. Daniel kept his cool. He was amazing.

'There's always people round here. Holidaymakers and stuff.'

'We're looking for three runaway children, two girls aged fourteen and a boy of ten. One of the girls was in the village shop this morning. Here're their photos.'

There was a silence.

'Yeah . . . I saw her. She dropped some money so I gave it back to her.'

'Sergeant, take the others and have a quick scout round . . .'

I could feel the panic rising.

'She didn't hang about though. She ran off towards Blakewell's Farm.' I could hear the urgency in Daniel's voice as the policeman came nearer the cave.

'Blakewell's Farm, you say?' He was right outside the cave. No more than two metres separated us. Through the bundle of scrub I could see his dark trousers and shiny black police boots splattered with specks of dirt and leaves. I had my arms round Re and didn't dare to breathe. I glanced over at Jamie. The whites of his eyes were wide and staring. He wasn't even daring to blink.

'Yeah . . . I'll show you where I saw her go if you want.'

'OK, come on then, let's take a look.' He called to his colleagues. 'Hey – this kid saw one of the girls.'

I breathed a sigh of relief. They were going.

'Oh and another thing,' the policeman said. 'Their dad might show up. He's absconded from prison . . . probably looking for them.'

My heart missed a beat. I glanced over at Jamie. Shocked and dazed as if someone had just hit him, he slowly turned and stared at me.

'It's all right,' the policeman continued, 'he's not dangerous, but we'd like him back behind bars.'

The voices died away but still none of us dared to move. Jamie was now staring down at the ground. After about five minutes, I slowly leant forward to peep out. I felt my arm sharply pulled back as Jamie swung me round.

'You told us Dad was abroad, delivering stuff to refugees!' He glared at me, his face buckling into anger and fury.

'I didn't want you knowing . . .'

'You didn't want us knowing where our own dad was?'

'Why's Dad in prison? What's he done?' asked Re.

'That stuff he used to deliver for Mr McCready on the quiet. It was all stolen.'

'Was he a burglar?' asked Re.

'Course not. He was only trying to keep us all going!' shouted Jamie. 'He wouldn't have done anything wrong if he didn't have to! He's our dad!'

Reddening, I remembered what happened in the shop.

'Jamie, I'm so sorry.'

'We could have gone to see him in prison if we'd known! I hate you, Vicky Davies! You're so bossy . . . and you always think you're right!'

Jamie leapt up and barged past me out of the cave.

'Jamie . . . no! Where are you going?'

'Anywhere away from you!'

'Jamie, come back! You can't just run off like this!'

'Watch me!' he hissed, jumping over the stream and disappearing into the woods.

Chapter 37

'I want Jamie.'

He'd been gone for ages. We sat on the cave floor. I had the tin with Peter in on my lap. I wanted to go outside to get him some fresh grass but Vicky wouldn't let me go anywhere.

'We've got to stay here, Re,' she said.

'I want Jamie.'

'He'll come back soon . . .'

'When?'

She didn't say anything. Her eyes were red and puffy.

'When Vicky?'

'I don't know . . . When he's hungry. He always comes home when he's hungry. You know that.'

'Let's go and look for him.'

'We can't.'

'Why?'

'Because there're police everywhere.'

'But we could ask one of them to help us. Mrs Edwards says if I get lost I have to ask a police lady or a policeman or . . . um . . . just an ordinary lady on her own . . . or a lady with children . . . or two ladies together . . . or if I can't find any ladies on their own or with children or with another lady then I have to ask a lady and a man but —'

'Rhianna shut up . . . please . . .'

'Nuckets to you.'

I turned my back on her. She hated that. I looked down at Peter. I touched his fur. He didn't move. I took him out of the tin and held him in my hands. His fur felt soft but his body was stiff.

'Wake up.'

I poked him again really gently. He still didn't move. I showed him the penguin but he wasn't interested. Vicky came over. She tried to put her arm round me but I pushed it off.

'He's just asleep,' I told her.

'He was really ill Re . . . Too ill to live. He's dead now.'

'He's not. He's asleep. You don't know anything. Jamie was right. You think you know stuff but you don't. He's just asleep because he's tired.'

Vicky made a big sighing noise then went and stood by the mouth of the cave.

I stroked Peter gently with just the tips of my fingers. When you're not well you have to be looked after.

Chapter 38

I left Re cradling the dead rabbit and crept out of the cave into the fresh air. I remembered those first few days after Mum died; Dad had shut himself away in his room but Re hadn't been upset at all. I bit my lip as I realised she just hadn't understood what it all meant.

There was no sign of Jamie. I wondered if the police had already found him. I pictured him sullen and cross, being driven back to the local police station, kicking the seat of the driver in front and trying to whack the policeman next to him. No wonder he was angry. He'd got a right to be. Jamie was only eight when Dad was sentenced and neither he nor Rhianna had really understood when Mrs Frankish told us all Dad was going away and we wouldn't be able to visit. The prison was over a hundred miles away. Writing 'no contact with dad' on our records was her cop out.

Weaving a fairy tale about him delivering supplies for refugees was mine. I know I should have told them the truth but somehow it had just seemed so much easier to change the story. Too easy in fact. They'd always trusted me to explain things to them.

I couldn't bear the thought of anyone finding out – especially Jamie and Re who both worshipped Dad. If Jamie had known, he would have immediately told his friend Sam who would have told his mum and then it would have been round the whole town in no time. Rosie would have heard and so would Matt and the evil Charlene Slackton. I'm sure Rosie would have been all right about it, although her parents sounded a bit posh – they ran some sort of furniture business – and probably wouldn't approve of Rosie being friends with some prisoner's daughter.

As for Charlene Slackton – I could just imagine her blabbing non-stop to everyone. And I mean everyone. That girl had a mouth on her the size of a small country and she wasn't afraid to open it and dish the dirt. Knowing her, we would have become the unfortunate spawn of an evil serial murderer. Exaggeration was her speciality.

Daniel didn't judge me when I told him where Dad was but Matt would have run a mile. Manky Matt. What on earth did I ever see in him?

But I wasn't just trying to protect Jamie and Re and stop others finding out. They weren't the only reasons I'd lied. It went deeper than that. Dad had left me on my own to look after Jamie and Rhianna. To be their mum and their dad. I was still angry with him for that.

I tried to push all thoughts of him out of my mind. It was his own fault after all. He'd got himself into the mess he was in. And I didn't ask him to come after us. He didn't have to. He'd been in what they call an open prison, where the security wasn't high and the inmates sometimes went out to do supervised work. But absconding must be really serious. He'd be in deep trouble when they finally caught up with him. So why had he risked everything to find us?

Then the simple truth hit me. He'd come after us because he still loved us and he still cared what happened to us. I felt a lump like a ball of mud stick in my throat. So what did I care about? With a huge feeling of relief, I realised that what Rosie, Charlene Slackton and Manky Matt thought about me didn't matter one little bit. What I cared about was Re, Jamie and yes, even though I was still angry with him, Dad too. And the only thing that mattered right then was finding Jamie safe and sound.

I went back into the cave. 'Re, come on. Let's go.'

She insisted on bringing the dead rabbit. She put it gently back in the tin next to her little penguin and covered them both with Jamie's T-shirt so they wouldn't be cold. We crept out of the cave, searched the woods for a bit and then followed the stream down to the lake. We were about to give up when I looked out on to the island and saw someone half hidden behind a tree. Re saw him too.

'It's Jamie! Look, Vicky! He's on the island!'

Jamie must have heard us as he looked over. Rhianna waved but he didn't wave back. He quickly turned away and disappeared behind a bush.

I ran down to the old up-turned dinghy wondering what to do next. In the distance we heard the sound of dirt bikes. I scanned the woods but couldn't see them yet. But they were coming. Coming for us. Coming for revenge.

There was no way we could get back to the cave in time, besides which we couldn't leave Jamie on his own. I looked down at the boat. There was only one thing we could do.

'Quickly, Re. Help me!'

Together we turned the dinghy over and started to drag it down to the water's edge.

Chapter 39

'Re climb in, hurry!'

I jumped in and sat on the wooden bench. I put the tin with Peter next to me. The roaring sound was getting louder. Vicky pushed the boat out and leapt in after me. Vicky took the oars and started to row across. She wasn't very good at it and we went all zigzaggy. I looked down and saw there was water sloshing in the bottom of the boat.

'Use this Re.' She untied a small yellow bucket from the inside of the boat and gave it to me. 'Scoop out the water and throw it over the side. As quick as you can.'

I did what she said but more came in. So I scooped it out faster and faster but it was no good. The water came up over my trainers, wetting my socks and the bottoms of my jeans.

They came out of the woods. They skidded to a halt when they saw us and started shouting and yelling. The girl was waving something. I stood up to get a better look.

'Sit down Rhianna!'

'Leave my Baby Emma alone!' I shouted.

'Yee ha!' yelled the girl and she pulled off Baby Emma's legs and arms and head. She threw them all into the water.

They bobbed up and down for a bit then they sank.

'Re please, sit down – we'll tip up!' Vicky pulled me back down on the bench.

'Don't think you'll be hiding in your lovely little cave any more!' shouted the girl nastily. She threw Baby Emma's body into the water.

The boy looked at the girl and they grinned at each other.

'Yeah. Somebody seems to have trashed it!'

They both laughed.

'It's OK Re . . . It's going to be OK,' said Vicky. 'Don't cry.'

I couldn't help it. I'd had Baby Emma right from when I was little. Mum bought her for me. She was my special doll.

Vicky looked over to the island and tried to row faster. Suddenly, with a horrible screechy noise one of the oars popped out of its holder. Vicky caught it just in time but she scraped her hand. It started bleeding. She just let the blood run down her arm and drip into the mucky water.

'Let Re row as well!' shouted Jamie from the island. Vicky looked at me then nodded. I stood up again. The boat started rocking. It felt really wobbly and I didn't like it.

'Ha! Fall in! Go on!' shouted the girl. The boy tried to throw Jamie's torch at us but we were too far away. It made a splashing noise and sank under the water.

'Hurry up Re!'

Vicky held out her good hand and I grabbed it.

The boat wobbled again and I nearly fell backwards but I got on to the bench next to her and she gave me one of the oars. It was better with two of us. It was like a race but with people swearing and yelling at us instead of cheering us on. Vicky's face was all white and she was breathing really fast. We were nearly there but the back of the boat was sinking lower and lower in the water and it was getting harder and harder to move.

At last the bottom of the boat scratched on the ground. We jumped out. The water came up to our knees. It was cold and muddy. Jamie rushed up to us and helped pull the boat up on to the grass. We paddled out of the water.

'We know who you are,' yelled the boy. 'Saw your ugly mugs on the telly.'

'Three stupid little runaways,' shouted the girl.

'What are we going to do Vicky?' I asked. 'I'm scared.'

'They can't get us out here.'

'Just let them try,' said Jamie.

I wanted to go round the other side of the island so the bullies couldn't see us but Jamie said we'd better keep an eye on them. So we sat down and waited. And waited. Vicky thought they might just go away if we waited long enough. They'd stopped shouting now and sat on their bikes staring at us.

I looked down at Peter. I was glad I hadn't left him in the cave. They might have hurt him too. He still hadn't moved. Then I had a horrible thought. Maybe Vicky was right. Maybe he was already dead.

I asked Jamie. He was watching the bullies in case they tried to swim over to us. He looked at Peter and nodded.

'Sorry Re.'

I thought hard for a moment.

'Mum's dead . . . but she's coming back one day isn't she?'

Jamie looked at Vicky then back at the bullies.

'She can't Re,' said Vicky really quietly.

'Never? Not even for a day or something?'

'No.'

'Not even for . . . five minutes?'

'No.'

'One minute?'

'No.'

'What about just to say hello then go again?'

'Re she's not coming back, all right. Never. Not at all!' said Jamie in his shut up or I'll whack you voice.

'But that's not fair!' I felt cross now. Nobody had told me that before. 'So where's she gone?'

Vicky and Jamie were staring at the bullies. They wouldn't even look at me. Vicky's mouth was all twisted up.

'Where is she?' I asked.

'Dunno. Heaven or something . . .' said Jamie.

'So where's that then?'

'Don't know . . .'

'Vicky?'

She shrugged. 'Up in the sky somewhere . . .'

'How can you live up in the sky?' I said.

Jamie and Vicky went quiet. They didn't even know. I

looked over at the bullies sitting on their bikes.

'I wish she was still here, not up in the sky, jumping around on clouds.' I had another thought. 'So why hasn't Peter floated up to the sky then?'

Vicky gave a big sigh. 'Look Re. Bodies die. They don't work any more.'

'But you said —'

Jamie was getting cross. 'Shut up Re.'

'I'm only asking.'

'Well don't ask. Not now. Just shut up.'

'But I want to know. Mrs Edwards says we should ask a question if we don't understand.'

Vicky looked at Jamie then said quietly, 'OK, so maybe it's just their spirit that stays alive.'

'What's that?'

'It's what's inside them. It's invisible but it makes them who they are – it makes them different from anybody else.'

I thought hard for a bit, then I stroked Peter for one last time. I put him back in the tin and tucked Jamie's T-shirt over him. I took out my little penguin and zipped him safely in my pocket. I fixed the lid on the tin really gently then I put the tin down between two tree roots and covered it with moss and leaves. Vicky was watching me.

'What are you doing?' she asked.

'I don't think Mum's spirit is floating around in the sky. I think that's just really stupid. I think it's here because this is her best place that she liked more than anywhere else. She told me. I'm leaving Peter here so they can be together.'

Chapter 40

'It'll be all right, Vicky. Don't worry.'

A huge lump rose up in my throat. It was the first time in our whole lives that Re had ever comforted me. I thought about Mum. What would she do if her spirit had been here with us? What would she say? I concentrated hard but felt nothing.

Rhianna's wrong, I thought flatly. You aren't here Mum, are you? We're on our own, tiny little specks alone in a great big universe.

I looked across the lake. There was a wind up now and small waves formed, making the water choppy and dark. Thick grey clouds were rolling over, covering the blue sky like a dull heavy blanket.

The beady-eyed girl was busy talking into her mobile phone. When she'd finished, the shaven-headed boy ran down to the water's edge and shouted over to us.

'Hey, saddos! Guess what? The police were really interested to know where you are. Looks like you'll all be going home!'

'Let's get out of here,' said Jamie, looking at the boat.

'But the bullies'll get us!' wailed Re.

'We can't, Jamie,' I said. 'There's a leak. We'll never make it . . . and I can't swim.'

'I'm not waiting for the police to turn up.'

He searched for the hole in the bottom of the boat.

'It's not that big,' he said, ripping a bit of his T-shirt then using the cloth to plug the hole. 'We'll be all right. It's our only chance.'

I looked at the old battered dinghy. I wasn't happy but Jamie was already pulling it back to the water's edge and calling to us to jump in. The beady-eyed girl started yelling.

'Oi! Where d'you think you're going?'

'Yeah – you can run, but you can't hide!' called the boy nastily. They both laughed.

'Nee-nah! Nee-nah! They're coming to get you . . .'

I took a deep breath. We had no other choice. Re and I climbed in the boat and sat at the back. I held on tight, praying that it would be all right as Jamie pushed us out as far as he could before scrambling on to the bench in the middle.

'It's not far, Vicky,' he said, noticing my petrified expression. Taking up the oars he started to row steadily.

There was still some water coming in and Re and I took it in turns to bale out. But as fast as we baled, more water flooded in.

He rowed harder, aware of the water but not wanting to acknowledge it.

It was gushing in faster now. The cloth plug had come loose and was floating around the bottom of the boat. I grabbed it and tried to put it back but I couldn't find the hole.

'Jamie . . .'

'We're nearly there.'

He was trying to keep calm but I could hear the note of panic rising in his voice.

On the shore I saw Daniel run out from the woods and up to the lake edge. Ignoring the jeers and catcalls from the two bullies, he started waving and calling to us. I waved back and shouted to him frantically although I knew there was nothing he could do to help.

'Daniel!' I yelled. 'We're sinking!'

The back of the boat was submerging faster now. With a sudden whoosh, water came flooding in over the rim and the boat dipped below the surface. For a split second, we were sitting in water up to our waists.

The boat wobbled.

'Quick, jump out!' shouted Jamie. 'We'll have to swim for it!'

Jamie and Re leapt out of the boat but I sat there frozen, unable to move as it wallowed and sank.

I screamed as I felt nothing but the dark inky water beneath me. It was deep down there. Very deep. Panicking, I thrashed my arms and tried to kick my legs as my head went under and I got a mouth full of dirty water. I coughed and spluttered, fighting my way up to the surface to gasp a breathful of air. I called for help but I could feel myself being pulled under again.

Kicking wildly, I fought my way back up to the surface but barely had time to cough out the water before I was going under a third time. As I went down, I was aware of muffled shouts and splashing but once underneath the surface, it was quiet and the water was dark and grimy. There was nothing I could do. I was being sucked down into the lake's depths, into its calm silence. An icy numbness spread through my body and it was then that I realised I was going to die.

I was sinking further and further down, lightly, delicately, weightlessly. Within the still quietness I heard a small, familiar voice in my head. It was Mum's. She was telling me I would be OK. But how do you know, I thought, how do you know? You're not with me – you're gone.

Then I saw her. Floating in front of me, vivid and real. She looked beautiful, exactly like she did before she got sick. A bright light glowed behind her. Her thick golden-brown hair shone as it fluttered silently above her smooth forehead and her cornflower-blue eyes with those long dark lashes looked piercingly at me. I could see the freckles over her nose and even the tiny pink scar on her jaw. She smiled at me and creases formed at the corners of her eyes. Her lips parted showing her teeth, straight and white and even. I felt completely and absolutely happy. Nothing mattered any more as long as I could stay down there with her, for ever.

I reached out my hand to touch her but suddenly from

behind me, someone grabbed hold of my T-shirt and started pulling me firmly and roughly up and out from under the murky blackness, away from Mum and the light. I watched, powerless, as, still smiling but becoming fainter and more distant, Mum slowly raised her hand and waved goodbye to me.

We burst through the surface of the water spluttering and gasping for air.

'It's all right, Vicky . . . I've got you,' I heard a voice say. It took me a few moments to realise it was Re. I tried to speak but the effort was too much. I clung limply on to her as she dragged me awkwardly through the water towards the shore.

Daniel swam up alongside us with Jamie. Their faces were drained of colour and both looked terrified. I wanted to tell them I was OK but just turning my eyes towards them was all I could manage.

Somehow or other we made it to the shore. Daniel and Re half carried, half dragged me on to the grass and turned me on my side. In one huge choking splutter I brought up litres of lake water and then gasped in a huge breath of air.

I looked at Re anxiously standing above me dripping with water. Mum had told me everything would be all right.

I forced out a whisper. 'Thanks, Sis.'

Re bent down and hugged me tight. I closed my eyes, exhausted with the effort. Daniel marched over to the bullies and demanded to borrow their phone. Surprised and unnerved, the beady-eyed girl handed it over and watched as he called 999 for an ambulance. When he finished he gave it back and told them to clear off. She looked like she was going to give him a mouthful but there was something in his voice, a different, new note. Something which said don't argue. She hesitated then, with a brief glance at the shaven-headed boy, the pair got back on their bikes and revved off into the woods.

I couldn't stop shivering. Daniel picked up his nearby jumper and put it over me. He sat down next to me as I lay helpless on the grass and waited. Slowly, minute by minute, I began to feel better. My breath came more easily and evenly. Gradually I stopped shaking. Jamie and Re were watching the opposite shore for any sign of the ambulance.

I looked up at Daniel and gave him a small sad smile.

'I'm going to really miss you,' he said quietly.

'Not as much as I'll miss you,' I replied, impulsively reaching for his hand and giving it a gentle squeeze. Daniel looked straight at me with those big soft brown eyes, then suddenly leant over and kissed me long and tenderly on the lips. He sat back and looked at me again but for once I knew I wasn't blushing.

'Sorry,' he mumbled.

'Don't be,' I heard myself saying. 'I've been wanting you to do that for ages.'

We could hear them coming from the other side of the lake with their sirens wailing and their blue lights flashing. The police car arrived seconds before the ambulance. But there was no dramatic capture. No big scene. We were all taken wet and bedraggled and wrapped in blankets to get checked out at the local hospital. Re was crying softly as we drove away, but I knew deep inside it wasn't over.

Chapter 41

Daniel's mum came to get him from the hospital but we had to stay there all night. They put Vicky in a room on her own but Jamie and I were in the big ward with lots of other children. It was really noisy and busy and hot and I couldn't get to sleep even though I put my little penguin on my pillow next to me. The nurses kept going into Vicky's room but when I asked if she was all right they just said she was doing fine.

The next morning Vicky was still asleep and Jamie and I were having our breakfast when one of the nurses came over.

'You've got a special visitor,' she told us. 'We don't usually let anyone on the ward this early – but we've made an exception.'

I thought it was Daniel but then a policeman came in with another man.

'Dad!' Jamie yelled.

I wasn't so sure. This man didn't look like our dad at all. This man looked worn out. He had a beard and his hair was long and his clothes were scruffy. And he was wearing a metal bracelet which was joined to the policeman.

'Is it really Dad?' I whispered to Jamie.

Jamie leapt up and threw his arms round him.

'Course it's Dad!'

I jumped up too and we both hugged him together.

'Steady on!' Dad laughed, hugging us back tightly with the arm that didn't have the bracelet.

'Am I glad to see you two!' he said.

'Are you in trouble?' Jamie asked, looking at the policeman who was standing next to Dad.

Dad made a face. 'Just a bit.'

'Did you run away too?' I asked.

He nodded. 'I was frantic. Couldn't think of anything else but finding you all. I was racking my brains trying to figure out where you might be, then I just had this weird feeling you were at Great Auntie Irene's. I hitched a lift.' He looked down at the floor. 'I didn't know she'd died,' he said quietly. 'I hid in the woods for a day wondering what to do next. That's where they picked me up, yesterday evening.'

'What was it like in prison?' I asked.

Dad started telling us about it. It sounded a bit like some of the children's homes but bigger and for grown-ups. Dad had worked in the prison gardens and now he knew about growing all kinds of stuff – tomatoes, beans, cabbages, potatoes, carrots, peas and loads of other things. Sometimes they let him out to work on a farm and that's how he escaped. He was supposed to be picking lettuces but he crept out of the greenhouse when no one was looking.

I told him about the stinky children's homes and Sarah and Paul and the baby. He went all quiet when he heard how we were going to be split up.

He told us he was sorry for what he'd done, he had been stupid and if there was anyway he could make it up to us he would. He said life was going to be better from now on. He wasn't ever going to be a lorry driver again and he was never, ever going to do anything wrong like delivering McCready's stolen goods.

Jamie looked at him. 'What about your whisky and stuff?'

Dad pulled a face. 'That's done with. Strongest thing I'll drink now is a cup of tea.'

'You're going to look after us when you come out of prison, aren't you?' Jamie asked.

Dad looked down at the floor again.

'Dad? You'll look after us won't you?' I said.

He looked at the policeman standing next to him. 'I will . . . if they'll let me,' he said quietly.

Chapter 42

'Vicky . . .'

I knew that voice. My head was thumping but I forced myself to try to place who it was. I couldn't understand why there were so many people round my bed – Re, Jamie and two men. I was afraid for a second, not sure where I was.

'It's Dad, Vicky,' came Re's voice.

'Dad?'

Puzzled, I lifted my head and looked at the men again – there was a policeman in uniform and handcuffed to him was . . . Dad. He looked a mess. I glanced at the shiny handcuffs as he shifted from foot to foot trying to hide his wrist behind his back.

All the anger that had been stored up in me for the last two years suddenly and completely ebbed away like the tide on a beach. When Mum died, Dad's world had fallen apart too. He'd been just like me, trying to get through all the bad stuff as best he could, making bucket loads of mistakes along the way.

'Dad . . .'

He looked at me uncertainly.

I reached out my arms. His face lit up and he lurched forward almost jolting the bemused policeman off his feet. Re sniggered and looked at Jamie who gave a small snort of laughter. The policeman frowned and tried to look dignified. I didn't care. I held on to Dad, hugging him tightly.

'I'm sorry, Vicky,' he whispered gruffly. 'I'm so sorry. I've missed you all so much.'

As hard as I fought them back, I could feel hot tears welling up in my eyes.

'I've missed you too, Dad.'

Chapter 43

Mrs Frankish came to the hospital in the afternoon and told us off five times for running away. I counted. She was really angry and said we'd generated a mountain of paper-work. Jamie asked how she got into her office if there was a mountain inside but she didn't say. She was too busy moaning. She never even asked how Vicky was.

When the doctor said we could go home, I was waiting for Dad to collect us but he never came. I kept telling Mrs Frankish I wanted to go home with him but her mouth went all thin round the edges and she said we'd be lucky. Vicky told me he'd still got a few weeks to go before he was allowed out of prison and besides that he was in a lot of trouble.

I wanted to go and stay with Elizabeth again but Mrs Frankish said we weren't allowed and told us that just for the weekend we were going to stay with a couple who lived nearby. She said they fostered kids in an emergency. Their house smelt of fried onions but it was nice and quiet and the next day Vicky didn't wake up till teatime. They had a big white cat called Egbert. He let me stroke him under his chin.

On Monday morning Mrs Frankish collected us in her car. She said we were going to go to a care home near where we used to live with Sarah and Paul. It took us ages to get there and Jamie was sick because he ate a whole bag of Jelly Babies. We had to have the windows open for the rest of the way.

We only stayed at the care home for a few days because two of the kids were away and we had their rooms. I didn't mind because it was a horrible place anyway but Vicky was getting really fed up with packing and unpacking our stuff all the time. Then Mrs Frankish told us she'd managed to find a lady called Sandy who could foster us for a few weeks. Vicky got cross and asked what was going to happen after that but Mrs Frankish just said there'd be a meeting to decide.

So we went to Sandy's next. She lived in a little house at the end of a long row of little houses. She didn't have a front garden, you just went straight in from the pavement. Mrs Frankish rang on the bell and a big fat lady in a swirly-coloured dress opened the door.

'Come on in,' she said. 'I'm Sandy.'

Mrs Frankish told us she had to go. She said goodbye then started walking back to her car. We went inside and followed Sandy down a long thin hallway. Hung up on the walls were rows and rows of photos of kids.

'Are these all your children?' I asked.

'Foster children,' she said with a smile.

'But where do they all sleep?' I said. I peeped into her tiny sitting room. How would they all squeeze in to watch telly?

'Oh, they don't live here now.' Sandy laughed. 'I've been fostering children for a long time. Over thirty years. Most of this lot are grown-up. Some even have children of their own.'

We went into the kitchen. It was a bit of a mess. There were bowls and spoons and packets of sugar and flour and some eggshells and on a wire rack by the oven a heap of lovely smelling cakes.

'Had a spare half hour before you arrived,' Sandy said. 'You do like cakes, don't you?'

Jamie grinned. 'Nah . . . Hate them.'

Sandy made a sad face. 'Oh blow. There goes my diet again . . .'

'I'll eat them for you,' I told her.

Vicky laughed. 'Not all of them Re!' she said.

'Thanks Rhianna,' said Sandy. 'You can help me ice them first, if you like.'

The cakes were scrummy and we had three each.

We went back to school the next day. It was nice to see Maxine again. Her mum had braided her hair with beads and she looked really pretty. I showed her the little penguin Elizabeth gave me and let her stroke it for luck. It worked because Mrs Edwards let us do clay all afternoon. We rolled out long snakes then wound them round and round to make little pots.

Charlene Slackton's going out with Manky Matt now. Vicky said they deserved each other. She doesn't like him any more – she likes Daniel now. He's been texting her and she texts him back. She ran out of credit yesterday so she rang him on Sandy's phone. They talked for hours and hours until Sandy told Vicky she'd better come off the phone before she wore it out.

After Vicky put down the phone it rang again straight away. She said she'd answer it because it was probably Daniel ringing her back but it wasn't. It was Mrs Frankish. She said the special meeting would be tomorrow at her office.

She told Vicky there would be some very important people there and we all had to be on our very best behaviour. I'd rather go to McDonald's.

Vicky asked her if we were going home with Dad after the special meeting and Mrs Frankish told her the issues were very complex. She always uses words like that. I think she makes them up so we can't understand what she's talking about. I asked Vicky what Mrs Frankish meant but she just got cross and told me not to get my hopes up. Jamie said not to worry. If they didn't let Dad look after us he'd whack them all in their rudey bits and he didn't care if they were very important people. Vicky didn't even bother telling him off.

She was really moody all evening and she'd started biting her nails again. She'd already chewed them right down to the pink skin and she'd even made her little finger bleed.

Chapter 44

That night was the longest I'd ever known. Sandy said we ought to get to bed early to be ready for the meeting the next day so we all went up at nine. Re fell asleep quite quickly, convinced that tomorrow she'd be back with Dad, but I lay in bed listening to the sounds of the night, unable to relax.

Niggling worries kept burrowing their way into my mind, churning up my thoughts and pulling them one way then another. By running away Dad had got himself in deep trouble. But had he also blown his chances of looking after us when he left prison? I just didn't know. Social workers were supposed to keep families together, weren't they? I sighed. I don't think I'd ever heard Mrs Frankish say one good word about him.

I turned over, trying to blank out the bad thoughts and

concentrate on the good. Us being together again. After all, that was what we all wanted. What we all needed. None of us wanted to be split up – we had a right to be together. It wasn't so much to ask, was it? It wasn't as if we were asking for the moon!

I checked my watch. It was four in the morning. Everything was quiet except my mind. That was driving me bonkers. It just wouldn't shut up. Then just when I thought I couldn't stand it any longer, I must have finally fallen asleep because suddenly I was back in our cave again . . . with Mrs Frankish. In my dream, she was done up as a witch – a full pointy nose and green skin job, bending over a cauldron, stirring a foul-smelling potion. I tried to ask her to help us, but she just gave a horrible cackle as she threw more bits of dead animals into her steaming pot. Then, thankfully, from nowhere, I heard Re's voice calling my name. I opened my eyes and saw her large moon face staring down at me.

'Vicky! Come on. Wake up! Sandy says we've got to get ready. We're going soon!' She turned back to her bed and taking her little penguin from her pillow, stuffed it into her pocket, for luck, she said.

It was eight o'clock. The meeting was at nine-fifteen. I leapt out of bed and pulled on my clothes. Downstairs, Jamie was already dressed and getting his trainers on.

Sandy took us by bus to the offices where Mrs Frankish was based. The journey seemed endless with traffic jams all the way and it was bucketing with rain, but Re didn't seem to notice. She was talking excitedly to Sandy about how we were all going to live with Dad and grow veggies and how she'd have a pet rabbit or ten. I glanced at Jamie. He was sitting completely still, his face the colour of concrete. His caterpillar eyebrows were knitted together in an angry scowl. He'd hardly said a thing all morning. Neither of us had eaten any breakfast.

The bus lurched to a halt. Sandy called softly to us and we got off, walked along the wet pavement then climbed the steps to an official-looking glass-fronted building. I gulped in some air. This was it. The place where our future would be decided.

Inside, the receptionist directed us to a waiting room where we sat for what seemed like a century, but couldn't have been more than fifteen minutes. Finally, a serious-looking man in a grey suit came in and told us to follow him. Sandy flashed us a small hopeful smile and wished us luck.

Chapter 45

The man took us into Mrs Frankish's office. It was cold and ponged of mushrooms. It had grey stripy paper on the walls and a big white board you could draw pictures on but nobody had. On the back wall there were shelves from the ceiling to the floor and they were full of books and folders and piles of papers. In front of the window was a desk with a phone on it. Mrs Frankish sat behind the desk. She was wearing a black suit with silver buttons. It had long sleeves and a high neck that looked like it might choke her. She didn't smile at us, not even once. She told us to sit down and pointed to some chairs with her bony hand.

Sitting next to her was a man with glasses and long grey hair in a ponytail and a woman with big sticking-out teeth who smiled at us all the time.

The man was looking through some papers on his lap. 'Where's Dad?' I asked.

The man looked up and stared at me over the top of his glasses. The smiley woman with the teeth turned and whispered to Mrs Frankish who whispered something back.

'Your father isn't coming today, Rhianna,' she said very slowly and very loudly with an even bigger smile.

'You don't have to talk to her like she's stupid,' growled Jamie.

The woman with the teeth put them back in her mouth. Vicky told Jamie to shush so Jamie gave her a shove and nearly pushed her over. I looked at Mrs Frankish. She was reading through the papers in front of her. Her nails were black and shiny.

'Jamie has a few anger management issues,' she said without looking up.

The man with the ponytail nodded but the woman with the teeth wasn't smiling any more.

'This meeting is merely for myself and my colleagues to assess where you'll be best placed in the future,' said Mrs Frankish.

The woman with the teeth said they'd better begin as she had another very important meeting in half an hour.

The ponytail man started asking us loads of questions about where we went and what we did when we ran away. Vicky did most of the talking, except when Jamie butted in and said something rude. Then they asked me what it was like after Mum died when Dad was looking after us.

'It was great,' I said.

'In what way was it great?' asked the ponytail man, looking at me over the top of his glasses.

I thought for a bit.

'We had jam sandwiches every night for tea. Or pot noodle. And we didn't have to have baths or clean our teeth or brush our hair.'

Vicky started to say something but the man stopped her and said he wanted to hear from me.

'Go on,' he said.

'And we stayed up really late.'

'Did your father allow that?'

I nodded. 'He didn't mind.'

'And why do you think he didn't mind?'

'Because he was already asleep. He'd have his bottle of drink then start snoring.'

Mrs Frankish made a clicking noise with her teeth then whispered something to the ponytail man. The other lady was busy writing things down. I started telling them about the day the men took all the furniture away and how it was fun sleeping on the carpet instead of beds, but I don't think they were really listening because they kept whispering to each other.

Then Mrs Frankish put up her hand and said, 'Thank you, Rhianna. You've been very helpful.'

She looked at the other two then said, 'I don't expect we'll need long to come to our decision.'

The ponytail man nodded. The lady with the teeth smiled her big smile again. She had lots of black fillings.

'So if you children will just go down to the waiting room for a short while . . .'

'Because I was helpful does it mean we're allowed to live with Dad?' I asked Mrs Frankish. She was shuffling the papers on her desk.

'Tell Sandy we'll only be a few minutes,' she said.

Jamie stood up and kicked over his chair. 'We're not going anywhere until you tell us we can live with our dad.'

'Pick that up on your way out, please Jamie,' said Mrs Frankish.

Vicky stepped forward. 'Jamie's right,' she said in a wobbly voice. 'We're not leaving.'

'And what's more I'll whack you all if you say we can't!'

'Yeah,' I shouted. 'And if you make us live somewhere else we'll just run away again!' I turned to Vicky. 'We *will* run away, won't we Vick?'

Chapter 46

Mrs Frankish pursed her lips and narrowed her eyes. I glanced at Jamie and Re's furious and expectant faces and slowly shook my head.

'No. I'm not running away again.'

'Vicky!' Jamie and Re howled at me, their eyes wide in disbelief.

'But we want to live with Dad!' said Rhianna.

'Running away again isn't going to make that happen, Re,' I said quietly. 'It's not going to solve anything.'

The toothy woman looked at her watch. 'I'm afraid I really do have another meeting, so if you could just leave us to our discussion . . .'

'Please . . . wait,' I pleaded helplessly. 'These are our lives you're deciding on.'

She glanced at Mrs Frankish, unsure whether to

ignore me or not.

'We will choose the option which is in all your best interests,' said Mrs Frankish firmly. 'Now, if you could go down to the waiting room for a few minutes, we'll make our decision.'

The ponytail man and the toothy woman both nodded in solemn agreement.

'You're going to split us up, aren't you?' My voice sounded odd, as if it didn't belong to me.

'We will have to consider all the relevant factors,' said the ponytail man.

'But you don't even know our dad,' I blurted out.

'We've heard what happened after your mother died.'

'But that's just it,' I said, my face burning red. 'Our mum *died*. She was very ill and she died and it was sad and horrible. But it wasn't just awful for us – Dad was totally devastated too. He was so messed up he just couldn't cope with looking after us at the same time.'

Mrs Frankish frowned. 'We know that Vicky, but —'

'But that's the whole point,' I interrupted. 'You only know about Dad *after* Mum died but you don't know anything about him before she died. You don't know what sort of dad he really is at all.'

There was a silence. As I searched their faces for some kind of positive reaction, I could feel my heart thumping against my ribs as if it might explode at any moment.

'Tell us then,' said Mrs Frankish gently, after a moment or two. 'Tell us what your dad was like before your mum died.'

Suddenly all those special memories that I had deliberately suppressed over the last couple of years came flashing back, jostling and crowding into my brain like shapes in a kaleidoscope.

I could picture us all about four years ago in the garden of some posh stately home we visited and hear our excited squealing laughter as we followed Dad, stretched out and rolling over and over down a grassy slope to Mum, who was giggling like a schoolgirl at the bottom.

Back home in our little kitchen, I could smell the rich tomatoey sauce bubbling on the cooker while we watched Dad's concentrated expression as he forked out a long skein of spaghetti from another pan and then deliberately wobbled it about pretending it was alive so he couldn't nibble the end to check it was done.

Out in our street I could see myself, much younger still, on my little pink bike – I could feel the wind on my face and the exhilaration sparking through me as Dad let go of my saddle and chased alongside me on the pavement shouting, 'Keep going, Vicky! Keep going!' knowing all the while he was still close by in case I fell.

And then one of my earliest memories . . . I was on our stairs in the dark, I could smell the pine scent from the Christmas tree as I wandered down crying from a bad dream and found Dad and Mum laughing together as they wrapped up presents in the sitting room. I could feel my cheek against the soft bumpy wool of his blue jumper as he carried me back up to bed whispering softly that everything was all right.

I felt a surge of happiness. But where should I begin? How could I explain our wonderful, funny, kind dad in just a few sentences? I glanced round at Re and Jamie – their expressions intense and serious. The toothy woman glanced sideways at her watch and fidgeted and immediately I knew exactly how to start.

'The most important thing to know about our dad is that he always made time for us. He used to work really hard, but when he got home it didn't matter if he was tired or busy or had tons of other things to do, he'd always find the time to listen to us, or talk about stuff or just play.'

'It's true,' interrupted Jamie. 'Every Saturday he'd take us to the park and play football or whatever we wanted.'

'And at bedtime he'd read us each a story,' Re added. 'I always wanted the same one. It's called *We're Going on a Bear Hunt*. It's really good. It's all about catching a bear.'

Another memory bounced into my head.

'Hey, remember when Jamie left the door to his hamster cage wide open?' I asked Jamie and Re who immediately grinned and nodded.

'Jamie came downstairs yelling that Mr Spud had escaped,' I continued. 'He was so upset. We looked everywhere, turned the house upside-down . . . Then Mum thought she heard a scratching noise in the bathroom. Dad checked and saw a little hole in the skirting in the corner so he peeled back the lino and spent the whole evening taking up all the floorboards. "Don't worry, Jamie," he kept saying as he got hotter and dustier, "I'll find Mr Spud. You'll see." And then finally he said he thought he could see something right in the corner by the pipes, so Jamie got the cage ready to put Mr Spud back in and Dad stretched his arm down and under and felt around and brought out one of Re's old socks! Then the nesting stuff in the cage wobbled and Mr Spud popped his head out and looked at us all as if to say "Keep the noise down, will you?" He'd been there all the time, fast asleep. And Dad looked at Mum and all the floorboards and all the mess and we thought he was going to explode but he didn't . . . He just said, "Well that's sorted then. Sorry to disturb you, Mr Spud," and laughed. He was so patient . . . Even when we were naughty.'

'When I was little I took all the eggs out of the fridge and dropped them in his wellies,' said Re.

'I made an insect zoo in his lunch box once,' giggled Jamie. 'Dad said he jumped a mile when he opened it because a load of beetles flew out in his face. But when he got home he didn't shout at me or anything.'

'I can only remember one time when I saw him really angry. And it wasn't with us,' I said. 'Re and I had just started junior school and they wouldn't let her join in the swimming lessons. Health and Safety or some stupid excuse. Dad was furious and he went up to school to see the head teacher. When he came back he didn't say much, but that evening he picked up Re's swimming costume and towel and told her they were going down to the swimming pool. He took her every Monday and Thursday evening for a year and taught her to swim himself. When they had a gala at school in the summer he made sure she was entered for it —'

'And I won three races!'

There was a loud knock on the door. It swung open and the man in the grey suit popped his head round.

'Mrs Trevellian – they're all waiting for you.'

The toothy woman darted him a vague look. 'I'll be with you in a moment,' she said.

The man nodded and went.

Mrs Frankish looked at her watch, then turned to us.

'I think you three had better go and find Sandy,' she said, indicating the door.

'But we haven't finished yet,' I said. 'There's lots more we need to tell you.'

Mrs Frankish ignored my plea.

'She'll be in the waiting room,' she said. 'I'll be down shortly.'

There was nothing more we could do. We trooped back to the waiting room and watched the smile drop from Sandy's face as she saw our gloomy expressions.

Rhianna started to cry and Jamie made a good effort pretending he wasn't about to.

But I just felt numb inside. Too numb to cry.

Chapter 47

Sandy put her arms round me and hugged me tight.

'What happened?' she asked, looking at Vicky.

Vicky didn't answer. She just shook her head and went and sat down in the corner. She pulled her knees up to her chest and hugged them.

'They told us we had to wait here,' I said.

'They don't want us to live with Dad,' Jamie said then he burst into tears.

'I'm so sorry. Really I am,' said Sandy.

'Are they going to send me away to that school now?' I asked her.

'I don't know Rhianna.' She bit her bottom lip.

'They can't make me go, can they? Not if I don't want to?' I looked at Vicky again. 'Vicky tell me they can't.'

But Vicky didn't say anything. No one said anything.

We just sat. And sat. After ages and ages the door opened. Jamie rubbed his face with the back of his hand. Vicky looked up. Her face was white and her eyes were staring. Mrs Frankish walked in.

Chapter 48

I tried to search her face for clues to our fate but she was avoiding our eyes, looking down at the papers she held in her hand.

'My colleagues and I have discussed things in the light of everything you've told us. And we've looked carefully at this prison report on your dad.' She looked up. Her expression was serious, severe even. I dug my fingertips into my palms and braced myself for the worst. 'Apart from absconding, it seems he's been a model prisoner.' She paused for a moment. 'We've decided to give him a second chance,' she said quietly. 'We're going to recommend that you return to his care.'

Shocked, it took a second for me to take this in.

'But,' she continued, 'this will only be for a trial period and under very strict supervision . . .'

Rhianna looked at me for an explanation. Jumping up I

yelled, 'We're going to live with Dad!'

There was a huge explosion from Jamie. 'Yessssss!'

Re squealed with delight. Jamie was leaping around the room, shouting and cheering and bouncing off the walls. Sandy laughed and hugged Re.

Mrs Frankish watched with a small, bemused smile on her face.

'Thank you so much, Mrs Frankish,' I said happily.

She turned to me. 'Don't mess up this trial with your dad, Vicky.'

'We won't.'

She patted my arm with her long bony hand, then without another word hurried out of the waiting room.

Chapter 49

We had to wait for days and days but then the letter came. It said we were definitely allowed to live with Dad. Sandy read it and told me. I wanted to go and pack my stuff straight away but Sandy said it was too early because we weren't going for another two weeks so we had to go to school as usual.

At school I told everyone in the Unit that we were going to live with Dad. Mrs Edwards said it was wonderful news and she was really pleased for me. She said I could draw a picture of Dad, Vicky, Jamie and me in our new house so I drew us standing outside a little white cottage with lovely red roses all round the door. Then I drew the garden with lots of trees and veggies growing in it and six chickens pecking on the ground and two pet rabbits in a big run on the grass. On the other side of our house I drew a big blue lake with a little island in the middle. Last of all I drew Mum and Peter's spirits on the island using Mrs Edward's special silver and gold pens and stuck sparkly glitter all round them both. I drew one of Mum's arms up in the air because she was waving to us. It took me until break-time to finish it. Mrs Edwards said it was the best picture I'd ever done and pinned it up on the wall.

At break-time Maxine and I were walking along the corridor when we saw Charlene Slackton. She was standing by the noticeboard with Manky Matt. She had her arms round his neck.

As we walked past she said to me, 'What you staring at Der-Brain?' She looked at me nastily but I stopped and looked straight back at her.

'I'm not a Der-Brain,' I said.

I didn't feel scared of her any more. Do you know, I just felt cross. She got on my nuckets.

I walked right up to her. I could see lots of spots underneath her orange make-up.

'I'm not a Der-Brain,' I said again.

She took a step back, and wobbled a bit on her high heels.

'Only joking . . .' she said.

Manky Matt grinned at me. Charlene turned to him.

'What's up with you?' she said.

'Nothing,' he said but he stopped smiling straight away.

When I walked home with Vicky after school I told her what happened and she laughed.

206

'It's not funny,' I said. 'Charlene Slackton's a bully.'

'Bet you she won't bully you any more,' Vicky said.

'She better not pick on Maxine either,' I said.

At the weekend, Sandy took us to see Paul and Sarah. Sarah had come home from hospital. We went in and Paul was smiling all the time and he said come and meet our new addition. I didn't understand what he meant but we followed him upstairs into my old bedroom with the new fluffy duck and rabbit curtains. Sarah was standing next to a wooden cot, and she was smiling too and holding a tiny doll wrapped up in a soft white blanket except it wasn't a doll. It was a baby. A real live baby.

'Her name's Grace,' said Paul, stroking her head with his little finger. 'Isn't she beautiful?'

I had a good look but I wasn't too sure. She didn't look a bit like Baby Emma even before I poked out her eyes. She had lots of tufts of black hair at the sides of her head but was bald on top like a little old man and she went all red and wrinkly when she cried. But Vicky said she was the most gorgeous baby she had ever seen so I had another look. Then I put out my finger and Grace grabbed hold of it and wouldn't let it go for ages but I didn't mind at all because her hand was soft and podgy.

Sarah let me and Vicky take turns to hold her. She showed us the right way so we wouldn't drop her and Grace wouldn't feel uncomfortable. Paul and Sarah were still smiling and I felt good because they were happy even though there was nowhere to sit down with all the baby stuff and mess everywhere.

'We're going to live with Dad again,' I told them.

'That's fantastic,' said Paul. 'But we'll miss you all.'

'Would you like another doll as a present?' Sarah asked me. I had told her what had happened to Baby Emma at the lake and she was sorry. She knew I'd had Baby Emma ever since I was little.

'No thank you,' I said. 'I'm probably too old for dolls now. Actually, I don't even believe in Father Christmas or that Mrs Frankish is a witch any more.'

I thought for a second. 'I still like little china penguins that bring you luck, though. I'm not too grown-up for them.'

'Maybe we could get you one of those then?' said Paul with a smile.

'No need.' I put my hand in my pocket and pulled out the little penguin Elizabeth gave me. 'I've already got one. And it's very lucky.'

I told them about Elizabeth and her big spooky house and how she saved us from the dogs in the garden.

'We're going to go back and see her one day. She lives quite near Daniel.'

'So who's Daniel?' asked Sarah.

Vicky went bright red.

'Vicky's boyfriend,' I giggled.

'He's not!' said Vicky loudly but her eyes were all bright and she was grinning.

Chapter 50

'Vicky?'

At the sound of Daniel's voice, I felt a net full of butterflies flap excitedly inside my stomach.

'How's it going?' he asked.

I could hear Jip barking in the background and wished they were both with me, right here, right now, instead of miles away down the other end of a very long phone line.

'We're going to live with Dad on Saturday,' I told him.

'At last . . . Bet you can't wait.'

'Sandy's been fantastic, but you're right. We're all really excited. And Re's had her stuff packed for over a week now.' Daniel laughed.

Then he said something I'd never expected to hear.

'I've . . . I've got some news too. I'm back at school now.'

'Really?'

'My parents sorted it and I went in yesterday.' He gave another small laugh. 'Nearly walked straight out again but I'm glad I didn't.'

'Why, Daniel? Why did you change your mind?' There was a silence. What on earth had happened, I wondered.

'Something to do with this girl I met.'

'Oh.' A sudden dart of jealousy stabbed me hard, instantly puncturing all my hopes and dreams.

'Vicky? You still there?'

'Um. Yes . . . course.' I forced myself to sound cheery. 'So . . . you . . . you met a girl then? I mean great, that's great. What's she . . . Is she . . . ?' I trailed off miserably.

'She's you . . . actually.'

Blushing like a beetroot, I punched the air, dancing in silent celebration. Thank goodness he couldn't see me.

'But . . . I never said you should go back to school.'

'No, but you sort of made me think about stuff. Face up to things I didn't want to face up to.'

'So was it OK? What happened?'

'It was all right. As much as double maths followed by double French can be on a wet Monday afternoon. It was weird being around so many other people. I suppose I'll get used to it.'

'What about the other kids?'

'There's a couple of lads I'm friendly with. We played footie together at break. They seem OK.' He hesitated for a moment. 'If . . . if anyone tries to take the mickey – and they haven't yet – I think I can handle it now.'

I thought back to that last day at the lake when I'd nearly

drowned and how he'd kept so calm and in control. I remembered the look on his face when he handed back the mobile to the beady-eyed girl and told her to get lost.

'You'll be fine, Dan. I know you will.'

'I meant to tell you,' he said. 'I went back to the cave. I found something on the floor.'

'What is it?' I asked.

'It's a surprise. When you've got your new address, let me know and I'll send it to you.'

'OK. Thanks.' I wondered if it was one of Re's Barbies or even the map we'd bought.

'I really miss you, Vicky,' he said suddenly.

The fluttering butterflies in my stomach went loopy, turning backflips in unison. If I were Rosie I could have instantly replied with something brilliant, witty and wonderful. But I'm me, so my best shot was to tell him the truth.

'I miss you too.'

'Come up and stay in the holidays,' he said urgently. 'It's not long away. I've already asked my parents. They're cool. They can even lend you our big family tent and camp beds and – you can all come and stay the whole week.' He stopped. 'I mean . . . that is . . . if . . . if you want to . . .'

'Daniel, I would love to.'

The next day at school I mentioned Daniel to Rosie.

'Hmmm,' she said. 'I've had my suspicions you've been concealing a romantic attachment.'

She leant closer.

'So what's he like? You really fancy him, don't you?'

'"Fancy", Rosie? *Fancy?* Exactly who have you been hanging around with, while I've been away?' I teased.

'Fancy is a perfectly acceptable word – I think you'll find the great William Shakespeare himself uses it in —'

'Come on,' I interrupted, taking her arm. 'Let's go and sit on the bench. I'll tell you all about Daniel.'

We sat down under the big oak tree and watched the younger kids chasing around like manic puppies. On the other side of the playground I saw Re and Maxine giggling happily together in the sunshine.

'I want to tell you something about my dad too,' I said. 'It was a big secret once, but it's not any more.'

Chapter 51

Vicky says the Prison Housing Adviser has arranged for Dad and us to live in a flat on the other side of town.

'But I don't want to live in a flat on the other side of town,' I told her. 'I want to live near Daniel in a cottage with a big garden and have chickens and pet rabbits and grow veggies with Dad.'

'We can't Re,' she said. 'Dad said we're really lucky to get this flat.'

'I suppose so. Maybe one day though?'

'Maybe,' she said. Then she smiled. 'It would be perfect, wouldn't it?'

'Except Jamie would want a pongy goat,' I said.

'No way!' she laughed. 'They eat all your clothes if you stand too near them!'

'What about Daniel?'

'He's invited us all up to stay in the holidays,' she said all excited.

'Really?'

'I asked Dad on the phone last night if we can go.'

'What did he say?' I asked.

'Yes . . . if we can afford it. And I'm going to make sure we can afford it. Seeing Paul and Sarah's baby gave me an idea. Now I'm fourteen I can earn a bit of money baby-sitting.'

'So we can go back to the island!'

'Yes but not in that tatty boat, thanks very much . . .' Vicky grinned at me. 'Hey, remember when we went on pedalos at that theme park years ago? You, me and Mum in one and Dad and Jamie in the other.'

'Yeah and Dad said let's have a race.'

'But we could only make our pedalo go backwards. And Dad was calling out instructions all serious but then Mum got the giggles and the more he tried to help the more she couldn't stop laughing, so we just went round and round in circles till the man called us in . . .'

'And afterwards she said it was the best boat ride she'd ever had,' I said.

We both laughed. Vicky and me talk about Mum a lot now. Sometimes it makes me feel sad and I cry a bit because I know she's not ever coming home but other times it makes me feel warm inside to think about her and remember things. I know she's dead and her body doesn't work any more but I still think her spirit is on our island. And so does Vicky.

Chapter 52

It was early Saturday morning and there was a loud ring on Sandy's doorbell.

'Vicky!' yelled Re from downstairs.

I glanced round our bedroom checking we'd got everything, picked up our suitcase (on loan from Sandy) and headed out to the landing. Jamie came charging past me and bounded down the stairs three at a time.

'He's here!' he shouted to no one in particular. 'Dad's here!'

He flung open the door and he and Re threw themselves into Dad's arms.

'Whoa!' Dad said, laughing as he lifted them off the ground.

'All ready, Vicky?' he asked me.

I nodded then ran over and hugged him too.

Sandy came up holding a large cake tin.

'Had a spare half hour,' she said, handing Re the tin. 'Chocolate flapjacks.'

We all thanked her, for everything, then loaded our stuff into the boot of the taxi. We said our goodbyes and Sandy promised to come round the following week for tea. We climbed into the taxi and, as it drove away, waved to Sandy until we turned the corner at the end of her street.

After driving for about fifteen minutes, we pulled up outside a tall block of flats surrounded by other tall blocks. We unloaded our suitcase and bags as Dad paid the driver. I looked up at the concrete tower. Dad glanced at me nervously but I grinned back at him.

'Relax, Dad. We wouldn't mind living in a cardboard box as long as we could all stay together.'

'Are we going to live in a box?' asked Re.

'No, we're going to live up there,' Dad pointed. 'Tenth floor.'

Jamie and Re tried to count the levels to see which was our flat.

'Come on,' I said. 'Let's go up.'

Inside there was a lift and stairs. The lift was noisy and it made an odd rattling noise, which scared Re a bit so she clung on to Dad. We got out on the tenth floor and looked round. There were four flats each facing a different direction.

'That's ours,' said Dad, indicating a tatty front door with *42* on it.

The front door opposite to ours opened. A lady in a sari came out holding a small child tucked on her hip and a folded pushchair in the other hand. She glanced at us warily.

'Hello,' said Re. 'We're coming to live at number forty-two.'

'Welcome,' she said with a shy smile.

'Thanks,' I called as she disappeared into the lift.

Dad turned the key in our new front door and pushed it open.

'It's in a bit of a state,' he said, picking up a brown envelope from the doormat. 'But I can do it up, bit by bit. And there's some furniture arriving soon.'

I looked round. Apart from a couple of suitcases and seven large cardboard boxes overflowing with saucepans, crockery, bedding and other stuff, the flat was empty. There was a little hallway, a sitting room, a kitchen, a bathroom and two bedrooms – a small one and an even smaller one. The people who lived here before us had liked bright orange, lurid purple and chocolate brown. A lot. Every room was decorated in a sickly mixture of those colours except for the bathroom, which was totally green – the walls, the floor, the ceiling – even the bath, toilet and sink.

'If you and Re share the bigger bedroom, Jamie can have the box room and I'll kip on the sofa, when it comes,' said Dad.

He explained that the prison had fixed up some training for him, restoring furniture at a local project that helped ex-offenders back into work and they were going to deliver some bits and pieces so we'd have something to sit on and sleep in. It sounded like the same project Rosie said her dad worked for when I told her all about my dad being in prison.

'But I thought your dad ran some really posh antiques business,' I'd told her. She looked at me and grinned.

'Whatever gave you that idea?' she said.

Jamie flung open a door in the sitting room.

'Here's the balcony!' he called.

We followed him out. There was only just room out there for us all. Standing forlornly in the corner were a couple of flowerpots and there was a washing line strung across the width of the opening.

'No garden, I'm afraid,' mumbled Dad.

'I can see a park!' said Jamie, looking out at the fantastic view.

It looked like a much nicer and better kept park than the one where we used to live. There were two tennis courts, a play area, football pitches and a boating pond with a little island in the middle.

'We won't need a garden, Dad, we can go there,' said Re.

I looked down to the street and saw a big van pull up. Two men got out with a girl. To my surprise, she looked up and waved. I did a double take. It was Rosie!

The men started unloading the furniture.

'Let's hope this lift doesn't break down,' murmured Dad as we all hurried down to help.

'Rosie!' I exclaimed when we got outside.

'Thought I'd come and help out.' She turned to the tall man. 'Dad, this is my friend Vicky.'

I looked at him and pasted on a smile. I could feel my face burning bright red.

'Nice to meet you. Come round sometime and pull Rosie's nose out of those books for a bit, will you?'

'Dad! Pl-ease!' hissed Rosie, rolling her eyes. 'You're soooo embarrassing!'

'That's what dads are for, isn't it?' joked Dad.

Rosie's dad and the other man, Dave, laughed.

'Ha ha. Very funny,' I said, grinning at Rosie.

Two hours later and our new flat had a sofa and two armchairs, bunk beds in Re's and my room and a small single bed crammed into Jamie's. We also had a fold-up table and four chairs, a wardrobe and two chests of drawers.

After mugs of tea and lots of flapjacks, Rosie, her dad and Dave left us to it and we set about unpacking the boxes, making up the beds and sorting out our stuff.

Mrs Frankish swooped in for her first visit later that afternoon. I felt really nervous and even Jamie was on his best behaviour. Actually, I've got a feeling she's secretly rooting for us. She gave Dad a cookbook and, despite munching her way through three chocolate flapjacks, she insisted on marking all the 'nutritionally correct' recipes with her green fluorescent pen. Re was definitely not impressed.

'I'm not eating that!' she said, pointing to a photo labelled 'Liver and Onion Surprise'.

I thought Mrs Frankish would get all huffy but she just glanced at the photo, gave a small laugh and told Re she didn't blame her.

It was only after Mrs Frankish had left that I noticed the envelope Dad had picked up from the doormat when we first came in. It was propped on a shelf in Re's and my bedroom, tucked behind her little china penguin – Dad must have put it there for safe keeping. It was addressed to me . . . and it was from Daniel.

Inside was the photo Great Auntie Irene had taken of Dad, Mum, Rhianna, Jamie and me by the lake. So this was what Daniel had found at the cave. I grinned. He'd managed to rescue the one thing that was most precious to us all, and apart from a small tear along one edge it was undamaged. I gently traced my finger over Mum's smiling face. 'It's never going to be the same without you,' I thought.

But deep inside I had the amazing feeling that a whole new chapter in my life was just beginning. And no matter what happened, as long as Re, Dad, Jamie and I were together, everything was going to be all right.